THE TEMPLE
OF
VITUS

CHRIS TURNER

CONTENTS

1: GRINNETH

Risgan, tawny-haired treasure-hunter, faces penury in the merchant city of Bazuur after devastating losses in forays to Lim-Lalyn. He is seeking his fortune elsewhere. His allies, however, have either gone their own ways, or fallen to foes or are sealed in dungeons—a rather unfortunate turn of events which has him waking from a strange dream at the hot air balloon station at Bazuur. He learns of his future daughter to be, also a wrathful 'Adjudicator of Time', who has adjudged him a 'Time Miscreant', quite literally a thieving meddler, after he unwittingly scavenged a certain piece of an experimental time machine. In light of such transgressions, the overlord Adjudicator wishes Risgan's head. Guarding an eerie sense of déjà vu, Risgan mulls over which direction to take: west or east, whilst he carries on his person two magic items: a youth talisman blessed with the granting of powers of youth or aging, and a wish bone purported to confer boons by wish alone . . .

1: The Vlon River

Risgan felt significant trepidation walking the gangplank to the balloon bound for *Ravel*. His effort to bypass the voyage for fear of the omens induced by his dream became overshadowed upon recalling the pitfalls of travelling these same roads by foot. Gibbeths, wizards, obscure flying foes... all haunted the outlying realms. He heard favourable reports of the town Ravel from the few people at the ticket booth, and on simple trust, decided to risk it.

The great red and white canvas balloon flared up, the gondola rocked... just like in his dream... He felt familiar qualms. Happily, the five balloon passengers were much different from those of his memory, and Risgan began to gain some confidence. The looming vessel gained height; he heard the fires roar and the fifteen-foot guide-birds, the grey-feathered and yellow-eyed teratyx, squawked at having their tethers pulled by the conductor. The lands swung below in a flush of green and gold.

Needless to say, a somewhat circumspect man by nature in regard to omens, Risgan did not strike up any conversations or gambling congress with his fellow travellers. For this reason, the voyage proceeded with a certain glumness. Perhaps it was befitting Risgan's mood, for he felt a changed man, or at least wary of gods, fate, and unseen forces, in memory of the disturbing words of the Adjudicator—or was it his daughter? Risgan gave a laconic laugh. Pure nonsense! A trick of the mind, a farce of imagination.

The conductor bawled out the names of the sites below: the Fallen Pillars of Lasinx, Sphinx Valley, Bisimen Keep, Ourtia Necropolis, the doomed City of Hugus, the Raging River Tivis, Bristlebax Falls, Fernamon IV's Parthenon, the cursed Obelisk of Duranth, and finally Mangor Wood. Once again, Risgan felt a noticeable pang tingle his spine. To traverse these menacing territories and dense brooding tangles as which wheeled below, would make Fadnar Forest seem a picnic...

The journey continued for hours, and leagues of forest passed underneath. Far to the east, a thin black river rolled north like an unfurled ribbon. Not far overhead patches of sunlight angled through broad covens of purple cloud.

Risgan peered up curiously as the canvas rippled. The weather was known for its capricious moods in these parts and not surprisingly, turned suddenly for the worse over the wood known as Mangor. A strong freak gust caught the balloon broadside, twisting it like a cork on the ocean. The canvas buckled, billowed, slid sideways in the updraft. The conductor compensated by smothering the fire and letting the balloon drop several feet. Down, down the carriage dropped while the winds raged above. The trees rose ominously to greet them, and Risgan thought, while peering over the rope-railing, to catch a slur of movement in those green cauliflower clumps of trees.

A strange whistling sound shivered from below. A projectile shot up

2

from the green expanse: a fire arrow that pierced the starboard teratyx, catching it clean through the neck.

Risgan felt his heart leap, his throat constrict. The beast flapped and died; its feathered hide caught on flames, flopping like a dead weight. It pulled the gondola sideways. On a dangerous yaw, Risgan plunged with the momentum of the carriage hard against the rope railing where he scrabbled to cut the strained leather reins holding the dying, twitching beast.

To no avail. The conductor efforted to tamp out the flames with his isk rod, flames that were eating the canvas.

"Cut the line!" he cried. "Or we die!" In his last frantic efforts, Risgan was pulled back with the gondola's sharp jerk—his blade could not cut the line in time.

There was pandemonium in the carriage as the gondola fell many more precarious feet. Another gust and the craft gave a perilous lurch slantwise. The trees below suddenly seemed like sharp spikes of death. Risgan braced himself for impact. Elbows and knees of the other passengers jabbed up at him with the force of truncheons and he tried to gain higher ground in the doomed craft, climbing up the rigging. A great tearing sound seared the air. The passengers flew like dolls. Leaves and splinters of wood thrashed about Risgan's legs, lashing and lacerating his skin. He was lucky to have one leg caught in a guy wire. It saved his life. He hung suspended from the certain crush of impact, upside down; his scored face was less than a dozen feet from grass and rocks, bobbing like a dizzy spider. His left leg dangled from the guy wire which was curled precariously around the middle branches of an old gnarled daobob.

The other passengers were gone, strewn—likely killed and beyond help in the sudden crash.

Yards to his side, the great grey teratyx hung impaled, with a quarrel ripped through its gullet, feathers still smouldering. The other beast had broken free of its harness and likely sailed off into the sky. Who had shot the arrow? It was clearly of primitive design. A thick painted shaft quivered gently with a ruffled fin of vulture feathers.

Wood savages! Risgan felt the urge to flee; the hunters would come for him, even if they expected no survivors.

Risgan gathered his wits. His hunting knife was still belted at his waist. He cut his ample bulk down with rapidity, sawing the keen blade along the wire's tautness.

The youth talisman was gleaming on the grass, like a ripe apple. He hoisted it gingerly, protecting fingers with the hem of his cloak so he would not be smitten by its enchantment. He wrapped it tenderly in his pouch. The relic hunter noted with distaste that the bauble was almost too easy to recover.

He collected the few of his possessions that he could find—pickaxe, calipers, flint and tinder—and scrambled on his hands and knees, muttering like a ship-wrecked sailor. The wish bone, gibbeth club, and the sum of his tools were gone.

In shock, Risgan loped to the edge of the wild clearing, mumbling an oath that he was a cursed man. He studied his surroundings. The ground was uneven, thick with coarse twitch grass and fungi. The young mandrake trees surrounding him were low and sprawled like twisted bonsai: thick olive green dwarfs with squat trunks. Between the twists of branches, dark holes peeked back, showing inimicable vistas stretching into the forest's interior. The old daobob had saved him, thrust up in the middle of the glade like a withered sentinel, a grandfather of ancient time. Remnants of the balloon garlanded its hoary branches, flapping like tattered flags. Raucous birds chirped on high, yellow bills voicing competitive squawks with the other birds of the forest.

Risgan assessed his wounds. They were minor, considering what he had survived. He faced facts. He was marooned in an unknown land, alone in the wilderness without guide, information or food. He must take action or the workers of this mischief would be collecting their fruits... even now he thought to hear a flutter in the woods...

The sign was no fiction.

A host of pygmy-like men came bounding out of the trees—four feet tall, if an inch, naked and painted all white with black dyes around their eyes and banded on all arms, loins and limbs. Several held spears, others gripped crossbows; belts of quivers lay strapped at their painted waists. Twenty of them foraged amongst the wreckage with predatorial competency.

A tallish giant strode forthwith out of the trees barking orders. He stood astride the daobob, looking up into the branches thoughtfully. He seemed to be the leader of the grim tribe. He pointed to the balloon and tattered wreckage and uttered an excited shout.

A half dozen of the pygmies bared knives and following the giant's order, took to the daobob. They were like monkeys, cutting down the ruin of canvas for their own needs, finding other items of utility—leather tethers, the guts of the teratyx which they dropped to the ground and let others either gnaw, or gather in fetid sacks. One pygmy fell out of the tree and the giant berated him, hoofing him, lifting him several inches off the ground. He ordered the victim back up the tree. This headman was easily seven feet tall, absurdly poised, so juxtaposed against the others who were half his height. His head was huge, a grotesque white oval skull, akin to a thing Risgan had seen carved in the primitive fanes of Durus or Phem in the far south. Risgan could not be sure, but he thought to discern the giant crouching down beside a clump of mushroom furze bent on skinning the hide of a figure who looked strikingly similar to Lolar the conductor.

The relic hunter winced, curling lips. Scavengers! If he were still slung in the tree... he shuddered to imagine what would have become of him. He wondered of his prospects now. Under no circumstances must he fall prey to the conductor's fate. He began to doubt the wisdom of his booking flight at the balloon way.

At last, he gathered up enough gumption to risk the forest. But which direction? The sun showed a hazy patch through a maze of mandrakes. He picked a direction that looked safe, and furtively cast a look over his shoulder.

He wandered in a daze, hacked through the tangle with his knife. Vines traced crazy arches overhead; trunks were closely-woven, often laden with epiphytes or creepers, forcing him to squeeze his way through the dim, green aisles. His hope vanished for a quick solution out of this nightmare; at best, the ghoulish pygmy raiders might make do with the bodies they had, not the one they sensed had escaped.

His choice of direction proved felicitous. Within a few hours he arrived at an unknown river, breaking out of the clot of mandrakes. The river was too wide to ford and the waters were black and fast-moving. The river, none too encouraging, veered wide, flooding the area with brackish water. A trio of crumbling statues of bygone tribal kings stood knee deep in murky water and weeds to shoreward. North and south, the watercourse drifted, like a great wallowing serpent, disappearing in a jade-coloured blur of foliage to the north.

Risgan looked longingly to the hither side, easily a span of two hundred yards. He recalled the malign charms of the Badan river, and bypassed an idea of swimming across.

Only as he made this easy decision did he see a flamingo or some other fowl, suddenly plunge underwater on the far bank. Risgan frowned. It had disappeared in a flurry of bubbles and feathers, as if some underwater predator had targeted it for a fine snack. He nodded to himself grimly. To make matters worse, the western shore, on which he was confined, was too rugged to pass on foot, north or south. Dark ferns rose like antlers in his path; stumps of old mongoose cedar and mandrake elm made miserable foot companions. He was in a pickle, and the retriever tried putting his wits together, thinking aloud for some time. Clearly, the river was his most expeditious route to safety and he felt no desire to backtrack through the savage forest and risk the domain of the pygmies and the savage lands he had recently crossed by balloon: Sphinx Valley, the Necropolis of Ourtia. He began crafting a raft of light timber, cut with his only useable tools, pickaxe and belt knife. It was tough going and the retriever expended several hours of hacking and whittling which gave but minimal results. He piled the largest branches on top of each other, strapped them together with rope foraged from slim saplings which he twisted and twined with precision. A crude sail of large manga leaves he onerously fashioned, knit together with tough strips of bark peeled from the old towering mandrakes. In this locale no undersupply of these dignified goliaths existed. He was in the midst of carving out a long pole to guide him in places near the shore when several fleet, loose-limbed shapes came darting out of the woods.

Risgan realized that cool aplomb was his only defence against the pygmies and retained an easy manner of industry. The crew surrounded him in a wide circle. He saw necklaces of human teeth garlanding their necks, front incisors filed like wolf fangs. Pale feet gripped the soil, flat and splayed for maximum springing. The lead scout burst out in a torrent of jabber which Risgan could not understand. A nearby savage clutched a crude bone hook in a hand, brandishing it menacingly at Risgan.

Risgan knelt at his task calmly and squinted up at them in peevish annoyance. "Here, now, what is all the fuss?"

"What do you do?" cried another who changed tongue in the broken vernacular of common speech. "We are the Aluka—fierce woodland raiders! We skin men's hides and drape them on our tents when we raid."

"This is only natural," concurred Risgan. "In truth, I build a raft to take me to the other side of this river—for hides."

The scout translated to his peers in excited gutturals. "The other side is forbidden! *Mitrim*—full of strange birds which revel in carving men's flesh and which dwell secretly in the forests of the Knug."

Risgan gave a raucous laugh. "Nonsense! The bank is within plain sight and I see no birds. Fresh hides are to be gained by the dozen, as I mentioned."

The scout peered with interest and suspicion. He translated to the others, and they stared from one to another, falling into a whispered murmuring.

"We know not of any river craft that has crossed the Yumina or survived," confided the scout, "only that we pluck sky craft that taunt us out of the sky with our fire arrows."

"That is an unsavoury practice... yet, beside the point. Look!—" Risgan beckoned to the two logs he had laboriously strapped together "—you see before you, the art of raft-building. This platform will become a giant ship."

There were murmurs of doubt, and awe, and the scout babbled on truculently to his mates. "We will summon Og, our leader, who will decide what is to be built. Our war-king roams upstream with a savage troupe of warriors hunting for survivors like yourself from the wreck."

Risgan discouraged such an act. "Such effort is unnecessary. Help me construct this raft and we will go to *Mitrim* together. You, me and your cohorts. Great merit is in store for all of us... and if you can bring Og hides, you will surprise and please him with some new wares. He seems a man harsh and unwielding of praise."

The scout affirmed the opinion and conferred with his tribesmen. There arose suspicious and controversial slurs of dissension.

"Efit asks, how do you know there are hides on *Mitrim* if you have never visited? Where is your craft? Why do we see you building one for the first time?"

Risgan scoffed. "Fools! Do you forget the balloon?"

More rumbles and whines filled the air. Eventually, the group consented to Risgan's scheme.

"Bring logs then!" commanded Risgan briskly. "We will need dozens of them to strap together to form an appropriate platform. Your saw-edged blades will work wonders here. Shake a leg, men!—before Og returns!"

The dozen pygmies set to work. Within an hour, they had, with the help of their efficient hands, strapped enough wood to form the initial phase of the platform. The raft, eight foot square was complete with a central mast and a small sail of Risgan's manga leaves and they pulled it out into the shallows. A group of primitives eagerly embarked on the raft anxious to cross. They stamped feet in wild unison.

Risgan cried out petulantly and held up a hand. "Halt! Are you forgetting the poles? How will we steer?"

There were fretful grumbles; ten men pulled out knives and began to whittle three stout poles from long saplings.

"You might as well carve out some oars too," suggested Risgan wisely. "Hurry!" he bawled. "Og will return in a brief time and our surprise will be spoiled!"

Grunts greeted the warning, but they promptly complied. Four crude oars were soon carved of the mandrake. The host jabbered on about the five foot long snargs with razor teeth that teemed in the waters of the Yumina river but Risgan gave an offhand wave, allotting little attention to such dangers. "There are gibbeths also who prowl the forest, yet we walk on land. Do we hide in caves all day?"

The savages had no answer for this and Risgan nodded in triumphant satisfaction. "The oars will do."

Several again sought to clamber aboard, including the scout, a fox-nosed hunter with long fingers and knobbly knees. Soon many of the pygmies were fighting amongst themselves as to who would occupy the best spots. Risgan whispered an earnest remark in the scout's ear. The scout dropped back in fervid conversation with his friends.

"These rafts are known to possess flaws," reiterated Risgan. "I will raft out for a small spell, only to test the craft for its river-worthiness. Should I fall to snargs... well, then I will be the sole sacrifice to Douran, not yourselves."

The lead scout agreed with the logic as did the others, concluding that the foreigner had a sound plan. With solemn ceremony, Risgan boarded the craft and poled his way out. "Wait, I will take these oars with me too—only to test them for their efficacy. Wait here, carpenters! Watch for my return. Not a word to Og!"

The relic hunter was well out on the river when the restless pygmies gave concerned shouts. Risgan gave a satisfied nod. He waved a florid greeting to the throng who huddled dourly about the shore like a pack of crows in black moods. There were indignant yells, pushes and shoves which grew to blows. At that instant, the saturnine Og chanced to storm the beach with his minions. The lead scout stammered his explanations to the war-king, pointing glibly at the outlander far out on the river, but he was picked up by the ears and dashed down by the giant. Og jumped on his back and the others bludgeoned him to death with clubs. The newly-arrived warriors stamped their feet and beat at their chests, gesticulating at Risgan with frustration and malice. Risgan smiled and gave back waves of thanks. Hollers and shrieks reached his ears as he poled across the dark water. Darts came plopping in numbers, too close for comfort and he hastily steered away. "Foolish heathens," he grumbled. "What a waste of weaponry."

Bad blood had been stirred and Risgan made efforts to dull his contempt. The acquisition of the raft had been an unexpected surprise and he applauded his ingenuity in procuring it. To work! he thought. Fair distance must be made before the pygmies could catch up with his craft, or somehow work some inconvenient mischief.

* * *

Risgan's craft was afloat, not a symbol of perfection, but one of utility and he poled his way cautiously down the shore, eye alert for unfriendly activity in the trees.

He saw none. Only jade dark foliage. The light slanted westward and merged with the brooding silence. Twice he thought to spy green-purple eyes peeking out at him, human eyes, red-rimmed and suspicious, but he could not verify it. That the pygmies made these northern extents their haunt seemed doubtful, even incredible. Risgan's suspicions were confirmed in the late afternoon when river folk shafted arrows at him, narrowly missing the flesh on his arms. One ripped his sail and rendered it useless. He kept far away from the western shore after that incident; only his pole guided him in the swift current.

Large fish surfaced often, some swimming close by with ribbed fins and pale orange eyes. Risgan guessed these to be 'snargs' and he huddled ever more cautiously toward the centre of the craft. Hundred foot high mandrakes choked the shoreline; some dangled out over the water like huge, poised ostrich. If he looked carefully enough, he thought to spy massive woven nests perched in those heights and sometimes the odd brown ape-armed quadruped climbing down with supple dexterity. Usilmars! Risgan had heard of these creatures, but never thought to encounter them. At other times, he thought to see strange conical dwellings lurking beyond the trees, with tufts of smoke rising from their tops, but he could not be sure from this distance.

The river widened and the current slowed. Risgan grew hungry. He did not dare risk a landing, for the dusk coming upon the land was the ripest for wandering prey. He bore his hunger, swallowed his apprehension and the crushing darkness that fell most swiftly. Few stars shone in the vast sky and the crescent moon was only a thin sickle shrouded in haze.

On the other side of the river, Risgan heard the squeal of victims, the pounce of gibbeths. He stared into the dark folds, a weave of menace. Mandrake trees with monolithic trunks and spidery branches stared back at him. Risgan shivered and hunched ever more sombrely in the centre of his craft. Gradually he gained confidence; by day he drew a line from some old coil he kept in his pouch. He tied a metal hook at the end and fished for walleyes and river gizza. When he dared land, he cooked his meat with furtive hops about the fire, fearful of what horror might jump out at him. He left immediately to the relative safety of the middle river. The forest was a thick mass on both sides with unknown menaces with eyes piercing through the shadows.

For five days he travelled in such wise, silently and alone down the endless expanse of river. One day he was surprised by a river tribe, when he made a secret landing and was confronted by a dozen men and women while he readied himself to bite into the fried salamander he had caught. They had crept on him like panthers, bare-chested and decked with shells and beads and gazing at him with soft indigenous brown eyes. They had long noses, brown faces, and wore oiled moccasins for footwear. Skirts of withe hugged their waists. These were no pygmies—but were of impressive height and sported long dark curly hair tied back in brown plaits.

Risgan realized that flight was useless. He assumed a confident ease. "What can you tell me of the lands north?" he inquired.

The spokesman, a tall angular-faced man with a hunting pike in one hand and sheaf of darts at his belt, responded kindly: "The river flows to the land of civilized men. From there our knowledge ends." Surprisingly, Risgan could understand their dialect. It was not too broad for his ears. "We know little of the city," continued the spokesman, shaking his mane of long, grey-shocked hair, "other than its name is Fugis, or Uksoma, as we call it in our mother tongue. Some of the residents' fishing boats come sailing up the river, only to fall prey to wading gibbeths or the merciless patter of our sleep darts."

Risgan nodded with barely-masked anxiety. "I know this place by dream. 'Tis surrounded on three sides by lake. Nevertheless, this comes as useful knowledge, else I would have paddled to my doom."

The native acknowledged the fact with sober click of his tongue. "There is no lake that we know of at Uksoma, only the river Vlon. My name is Nalsi, Chief amongst these proud peoples of the Fuzuli. And who are you?"

"Risgan, Relic Hunter of Zanzuria—and it seems—" with sardonic reflection "—somewhat of a vagabond these days on a forced mission."

The chief nodded with sober forbearance. "How came you so far on such a rude craft? This mishmash of wood should have sunk days ago."

Risgan admitted as much. "I stumbled across savages far upriver, small white pygmies. They cowered under a hulking leader of theirs, a certain Og with a skull head. Under my guidance, we built this raft together, in search of bounty on the hither side of the river. Before I could show them boons, they fought amongst themselves like badgers for who was to go, and I was forced to flee on this raft to escape their poisoned arrows."

The chief nodded sadly. "These are the Aluka and it does not surprise me. A horrid lot! We steer clear of them. They strip men of their hides and use them for grisly purposes. Og will one day come to ruin adhering to his barbaric principles. In fact, it is said the gods hated the Aluka so much, that they made them all small as monkeys, but I suspect it is only the green furze they eat so rapturously with their meat."

Risgan did not find it unlikely, muttering that he had some experience with Og and the savagery of their hide-stripping.

The chief grunted tersely and made no supplementary comments. "Well, you are amongst friends here, Risgan. Rest assured. We smell hostility and dark magic in weak men, of which you are not one. Come! We invite you to our village, unless you prefer dining on salamander alone?"

Risgan gave a grateful laugh. With cheerful camaraderie the group escorted the wanderer to their meagre settlement, which as it turned out, was constructed in a U-shaped glade hewed from the wood itself, and rested only a few furlongs north. The tribe made their location downriver, set in the interior of a dense dark green wood they called *Ferna*.

A circle of rude straw and mud huts dominated the village. Woods encroached to the back and a muddy pool lay to the side where women were bathing their children. An ancient fire pit ranged in the centre of the common area, surrounded by a bed of soft sand on which dancers and entertainers could gambol. Risgan saw the pale bellies of two dozen dugouts upturned down by the shore. He praised his luck for finding these river people and not barbaric pygmies. Toddlers frolicked in the glade with wooden toys of carved animals; some women transported jars of seeds and fresh water on their heads. A sinister shrine lurked at the perimeter of the encampment mounted with animal skulls replete with gaping mouths leering into the depths of the forest, a sight which caused Risgan a grimace.

A feast was set in order; a hustle and bustle came to the common ground. Men went out with spears to return from a quick hunt with fresh ibex and baskets of herbs. Day was turning to dusk; orange cloud darkened and an eerie glow descended over the forest.

A strange, somewhat sinister man gave Risgan a queer look as he approached. He was tall, long-legged, a barefooted individual garbed in a weave of tanned river reeds from chest to knee. He held a spiral cane of mandrake wood in a fist and stared shamelessly at the outlander. The fetish was etched with charms, fish scales and strange stones, jingling when he thrust it in the ground at the retriever's feet. "I am Xoltux, Village Shaman and Spirit-chaser," he announced proudly.

"A worthy position. I am Risgan, Retriever of curios, not unlike those embellished on your staff, minus the fish scales, of course."

The shaman ignored the remark. He motioned to Nalsi's private tent-hut. "The chief's wife is ailing and noise is forbidden. Nalsi is distraught." Risgan saw the woman lay apart in an open tent on a soft bed of leaves. The chief knelt at her side, clutching her limp hand, inviting Risgan to greet his beloved and share with him his anguish. Risgan obliged. The woman's breath ran in ragged gasps; a demonic fever seemed to rack her body, giving her face a greenish cast. Her upper lip trembled, her body lay drenched in sweat. Rivulets of sweat ran down her sopping scalp to soak her long silver hair in gleaming beads. Risgan was moved and found she could only glimpse him through one cloudy eye, but he saw, in that wilful gaze, that her spirit was strong.

The shaman, Xoltux, came up behind him and spoke in a commanding tone: a serpent's voice, sweet as mandrake sap. "Spirits have infested the lady Varwa's body! Filled it with ague, perhaps a large forest troll or swamp sloth. We comfort her as we can, but she cannot last for too long." The spirit-chaser knocked his macabre charm cane thrice on the ground. "So it is told to me by the forest gods."

Risgan nodded, unmoved by the shaman's pretentious speech. He was somewhat taken to pity for the old woman into whose eyes he peered again. Hope glistened there. Struck by a flash of insight, Risgan recalled the kindness of the service the river people had proffered him and decided to take a risk. The shaman had departed with the chieftain to confer in the glade and Risgan snuck back to the hut and thrust the youth talisman's brilliant curve into the woman's trembling palm. "Here! Do not be afraid!" he whispered.

The gem flared. He watched it as with a sudden inexplicable glow, the woman's eyes lit with a striking blueish light, and Risgan started, for it was the sign of some miracle at work. He left the talisman in her palm for some seconds before he pulled it back sharply. Clearly, the magic had done its work. He thrust the thing deep in his cloak. It would only cause him woe if he were not careful. He gave a satisfied nod. Unknown to him, the shaman had glanced back, and when he saw the foreigner bending over the chief's wife gripping a strange object, he had rushed over to investigate.

The shaman stood menacingly over the two, a shadow taller than death. He gazed in disapproval. He threw out a gnarled hand and pulled the retriever away. "Here, foreigner! This is not your place. What do you do?"

Risgan had already concealed the talisman in his pouch and did well to give an innocent exhalation. "It looks like bad weather tonight, Xoltux; I think we'll have to batten down."

The shaman gave a rancorous grunt. He looked at Risgan with utmost suspicion. A strange mistrustful smirk polluted his proud, gloomy face as he looked down upon the ailing woman. She seemed to rest peaceably without the ragged gasps. With no large compassion, the spirit-chaser prodded Risgan back to the fire where the common glade was lit up with torches.

Risgan was prompted by others to drink a foul brew: a mix of herbs and alcohol, though he secretly suspected it came from the large vat he had spied earlier from which they had poured snake heads and vole feet. The shaman assured their guest that the beverage was harmless, conducive to 'sharpening the mind' and 'bolstering the senses'. It also provided the ability to separate truth from illusion.

"No doubt, true," remarked Risgan.

"There is no 'doubt'," snapped the shaman with a trace of haughtiness.

Risgan found simple truth in the avowal, for he saw the trees around him weave in symmetry, like moths and spiders in flight, and the village figures dance like fairies, growing tall and thin and crooked and crouching like grasshoppers. Meanwhile strange domesticated forest dogs continued to rove about the common glade like boars, tearing at hafts of meat that the villagers had tossed down. Their barks and snarls grew unruly. Women danced around the fire with more abandon now while men told unearthly tales of the forest. There was laughter and light-hearted challenges, jokes and repartee. All sat cross-legged on the sand or lounged on low couches made of antler and vine. Under the influence of herbal brew, Risgan was entertained by the newness of it all; the chief garbed him in the gown and vest of the visitor, black owl feathers dipped in fish fat and woven with leather thread. He invited him to share an anecdote or two of his own. Risgan regaled the villagers for an hour speaking of his exploits with the bottled sorceress Afrid and a masked marauder and the fat patron, Zemore at Bazuur, who were either dragged to the donjon or strapped to the back of a direful isk.

"You have seen these isks before close up?" whispered several in awe.

"None other," Risgan answered modestly.

Not wishing to overstep his bounds, he turned the podium over to Narsi. "And what of you, wise Chief? How did you come to be the leader of this fine people?"

All leaned back, awaiting the chief's words.

The chief spoke: "We are an old race, going back to the time when the moon was a huge stone owl flying across the night sky, rather than the dead egg it is now, wobbling in its predictable course. My people have inhabited the *Ferna* forest since time immemorial. We were old when the isks were young! And you, Relic Hunter?" Nalsi asked curiously "—you seem a youngish man for all these escapades and capers you speak of."

Risgan proffered a small chuckle. "'Tis not easy to explain, Chief—" Nor was it easy to explain his fortune of youth. He had squinted at his reflection in the river not a day ago, and looked over a decade younger than when he had left Zanzuria.

The chief laughed. "You are a honest man, Risgan, and I will tell you of our people. They flew from beyond the sun. Few from beyond the woods know that after Bezran the Great slew the Great Gibbeth, our clan came into its empowered years, and this was a millennium ago. The Great

Gibbeth had been stalking men for moons beyond memory. Ozran was our first leader; he was christened 'Elder'. The moon rose and fell in flights of fancy and the Wise Owl fled from behind the gibbous moon to swoop down upon us and cover the forest with its magical grey wings. An age of shadow came over us. Our skin grew dark and blood-like as you see. We lived in fear, while dark things crept from the woods and bred, but the old owl finally melted away over the ages of sun and we were bathed in light once more to hunt and fish and roam the forests in freedom. We stayed free of the river, never crossing its banks to explore the other side where our ancestors claimed the Wise Owl's kin would someday be reborn and come to shroud us with their darkness."

Risgan frowned in surprise. "The forest is not dangerous then as it used to be since the owl's disappearance?"

The shaman gave a great hoot. "The only reason we are not descended upon and mauled by gibbeths is because I have protected these grounds with strong and powerful magic. Regard the fane, the gibbeth skulls!"

Risgan took solemn notice of the shrine. It wound away to the forest with its twisted skein of antlers, bone and horn.

"If you look closely," Nalsi stated shrewdly, "you can see the one-eyed fanged statuary with the furry appendages, a fanciful interpretation of a kodo in heat. During daylight hours, the forest sleeps and the kodos lie dormant."

"But at night," the shaman roared, "the ghosts haunt and the owl flies!"

Risgan muttered a note to strap himself into bed, or curb his nasty habit of sleepwalking.

The remark earned several chuckles. Several of the younger members rose to pour Risgan some more qualack.

The chief ignored the merriment. "Xoltux is my older half brother who chose the path of spirit-chaser well before I was born. It was before I was slated to rule the clan, given the elemental nature of our spiritual and practical disciplines."

Xoltux absorbed the information with masked displeasure. "Nalsi is wise as men go," he intoned grudgingly, "perhaps not as clever or all-seeing as me, but to his credit, the shaman always advises the chief on policy-making regarding the future of the clan. Only yesterday I opened the breasts of two small owls and discerned a long winter and the deaths of many men."

"This is dispiriting news," observed Risgan. Secretly he believed little could be had in butchering owls, nor did he tender much faith in the auguries of magicians or mystics. "For a fact I know the Pontific of my own people hired a magician-divinator who wrongly forecasted the conjoining of the seven clans who signed the treaty of Marsis, if this is any reflection on the nature of divinations."

The shaman curled his lips into a thin sneer. "It seems that your 'divinator' needs to take lessons from a person of repute, like myself. He needs somebody of quality versed in the old traditions."

"He would be better off," agreed Risgan, "studying the old wisdom, but I am not one to judge or counsel men on paths who are wiser than myself."

"Well said!" cried Nalsi, thumping Risgan on the back. "You are a wise and sensible man! Do you care for another nut-cup of this qualack?"

"Gladly." Risgan tipped his cup.

So the night passed in less troubled tones with the slosh of forest ale, dulcet songs and convivial banter. Two fellows brought out a queer instrument with double necks of four goat-gut cords and plucked the strings while a third bent low to slap the bottom like a drum. A sweet, haunting melody filled the glade, accompanied by the women's humming a soft chant. Risgan swayed to the music, obviously infected with the qualack, while the villagers caroled on in approval.

The night was old. Many had retired to their huts and a young maid, beguiling to one's sight with doe eyes and buxom figure, was pushed toward Risgan as an offering for his leisure. Her bare-skinned legs glistened with a golden sheen under the flickering firelight; her long narrow face showed an expression of alert intelligence rather than submissive fear or the bleak surprise of a coerced maid.

Risgan arched back in good humour. He was relaxed by the brew. Not wishing to upset or even offend the forest people, and taken to languor, he went on to enjoy several leisurely hours in the comfort of the private tent aside the chief's.

He emerged hours later in a state of lordly ease, admiring the moonlight while he relieved himself. Needless to say, he returned to his woven-reed bed, where he slept in docile comfort as he had never before.

* * *

Come morn, the chief and others gave Risgan gifts of furs and a small dugout to replace his deteriorating raft; also, a large black and red octagonal charm, mounted on a blue runestone, which the chief personally hung on a feathered chain about the adventurer's neck.

Risgan, touched by the act, blinked warm gladness and gave them all the two small clear-silver beads that he still had in his collection—items once worn by a faraway, long-dead princess, so he claimed. He entrusted the raft to the village seniors who consigned it as an amusing toy to the younger members of the tribe. Boys and girls of indeterminate age dragged it out in enthusiasm to a place far out in the river to be the object of their war games, whistling and hooting. Several reined in on dugouts and pelted mud and rocks at it from their small craft.

"They are a rambunctious lot," chuckled Nalsi. "Steer clear of the far shores, Risgan, and you will avoid the bloodthirstiest gibbeths," he advised solemnly.

"I shall."

The relic hunter turned to leave but observed there was a furor in the glade in the vicinity of the chief's hut. Such disturbances could only portend bad tidings. He frowned. Xoltux came charging out with a livid sneer on his face and mouthing words in a tongue that Risgan could only understand as anger. It was obvious that grave news of Risgan's deeds touched the kinsmen. Risgan hurried his untying of the craft. Several of Xoltux's staunchest supporters surrounded the chief, like guards.

Risgan made efforts to steer his dugout out past the reeds, but he was not far out on the river, when shouts and beseeches drifted to his ears. Xoltux had accused the outlander of being a magician, and that the shaman had personally witnessed him manipulating an evil stone upon Varwa the chief's consort, and now she was young again. "It's witchcraft. I saw him, brother! Your wife is cursed too. She has bypassed the natural course of her life! When she should have passed to Dayagubuf, the compassionate spirit, she has now gone on to defy destiny!"

Nalsi was confused and thunderstruck.

The spirit-chaser rallied his supporters; he pointed two fingers out on the river, saying that the detestable foreigner had poisoned them all and their way of life. "He has averted the laws of nature! We must capture this evil doer and the poisoned thing in his pouch, which we will bury. He along with it."

Nalsi was overwhelmed by the news and Risgan gritted his teeth. Silent rage gripped him. He was convinced that the fanatic shaman only hungered for the relic himself—to use it for his own depraved ends.

There was a fierce debate amongst the tribesmen over what action to take. A strange clicking dialect filled the communal glade—ominous possibilities followed.

Risgan cursed the complication. The spirit-chaser was an evil plague, and the retriever paddled with fury. The elderly matron had clutched the relic for too long, he knew. Even from this vantage he could see her being led by the elbow by a handsome young man, Valfri, her son, looking no older than herself. Risgan gaped, He could not help but wonder anew at the magic of the youth talisman. The relic was cursed, even when it was promptly used for good purpose.

The adventurer withdrew the bauble and with cautious trembling hands, wished to fling it far into the depths of the river. But he stayed his hand. The feeling alarmed him. Almost as from a dream, he felt the gem beckoning him, drawing him closer, as if whispering its need for other purposes—which were beyond his knowledge.

The chief, flustered by all this uproar, stood stunned for several moments. He was nonetheless ecstatic at the sight of his healthy wife, now so radiant and youthful that he ran to embrace her, showering her with kisses. Disbelief shone in his eyes. Looking back at the stern shaman, the chief seemed torn. Between loyalty for his brother and gratitude for the outlander who had miraculously healed his beloved.

Xoltux grinned; he and his own followers did not need the chief for their purposes. They rallied together and pursued Risgan in their dugouts. The shaman was at their head. The swish of projectiles whizzed past Risgan's head and closed in the dark water cut by the hull.

Risgan ducked low; he could feel the thud of projectiles rocking the gunnels in alarming frequency. Sharp obsidian tips pricked through the weave of his heavy cloak, some through the fine wicker-work of the dugout. Poison darts! Bridling with anger, Risgan gathered his courage. He rowed like a madman till his arms were near spent. The effort was in vain—the shaman's dugouts were sleeker and pulled by stronger arms than his. The flotilla bore down on him without remorse. Providence was on its way for the chief had mustered his own force which flew out on their boats, at least equalling Xoltux's.

Risgan gave a snarl of satisfaction. Out in the wide bay of sparkling jade waters, there ensued a furious battle, each craft dragged along in the lee of the Vlon's current. The shaman's flotilla was forced to turn hither and face the new resistance.

Poison darts flew like hail stones. They thudded into naked breasts; boats banged together, ramming enemy craft and shrieks fled across the bay, rocking the wide river. The whack of clubs on bone and the jabbing of spears and men jumping from boat to boat poisoned the air. Risgan flinched in horror. He hung his head low, hating what he witnessed.

Gratefully, he looked back to witness the full deadlock and a space of diminishing violence. He paddled stealthily closer to the shore, moving downriver in the fierce current. A half mile later he beached his craft in a nest of mandrake roots. He struck out on foot, hoping to avoid detection from the water, also later to regain his craft when the furor had died down. He thought long and hard, caring little for the cuts and scrapes he accumulated as he swept into the dark trees.

The shaman had steered away in disgust, avoiding the inconvenient dragnet. Now he was little interested in the battle with Nalsi and was more concerned with Risgan. Following the relic hunter with stealthy proficiency downriver, he saw the beached, half hidden dugout and gave a mirthless sneer.

Gasping for breath, Risgan looked around the clot of trees with anxious intent. He sensed the pursuit of an enemy who knew the forests better than he. What to do? Keep running?

Another foe was afoot. Perhaps an ulsimar or gibbeth? The relic hunter shuddered. He might escape his predators, if he did the unexpected thing... which entailed plunging deeper into the forest... The enemy of the dismal wood might be his saviour.

Risgan may have underestimated his enemy. Xoltux, for the shaman he was, seemed to be a ghost himself, plodding along the loam with half the effort, knowing all the secret ways of the forest. Risgan made good progress, hacking stealthily with his knife through vine trailers and spidery knots of mandrakes, though he felt the eyes of predators on his back. He skirted a few unnerving bubbling mud pools, which he thought to be quicksand. These traps had an evil cast to them and he thought to sense a large shuffling shape following his heels several bowshots back but when he stopped and peered, the menace was gone—or was either so still as to meld with the eerie forest. Risgan shuddered in doubt; he proceeded with utmost caution.

There was much Risgan saw in this land that was beguiling and terrifying: red-belled flowers whose mouths seemed to pine for flying insects; long cornflower stalks which swayed to the gentle movement of passing feet and an eerie cognizance; twice, he stared aghast as yellow, barbed vines dipped down from branches and attempted to coil about him. He slashed out with his knife and blundered on like a drunkard, half stumbling in consternation, dangerously close to another noxious mud pool.

Risgan halted, bereft of breath, almost abreast an impenetrable wall of mangor cedar. The shaman had thrown his voice, unknown to his knowledge and a vicious growl came bounding from the brush.

Risgan fell back springing in dismay. The threat of gibbeths this far north loomed foremost in his mind. He clambered in a different direction, wherein came yet another roar of immeasurable savagery.

Two gibbeths? Risgan stood stock still. He bolted in an opposite direction. Stumbling about in confusion, he forged his way between two mossy stumps. He halted again, looking frantically from side to side. He seemed sandwiched between alternating sounds of menace. Risgan's head spun. Oblivious to the shaman's ventriloquist ability, Risgan discovered himself now wedged before a wall of rippling green spider vine and a long garden of bubbling quicksand. He turned in dismay, feeling defeat heavy at his heels. He tried to back out, heel his way to safety—but no! his luck had run out... There was nowhere else to go.

The shaman approached on quiet feet. He stroked his magic stave, an impressive talisman, which glinted eerily in the dim afternoon light.

"Well, a convenient catch," he gloated. "We have with us a leghorn, green to the ways of the *Ferna*."

Risgan feigned defeat; he did well to let his shoulders sag. "You are wise and crafty, Xoltux. It seems as if you have me at a disadvantage; well, what is it you want? My death or the stone?"

"Why not both? Your body, conveniently undiscovered, would not be wont to tell tales; withal, the stone would provide my enterprise with another curio to keep the weak, artless fools of Nalsi's in thrall of my ambitions. One can never have enough talismans, I say," he chuckled.

"'Tis nothing more than I suspected," growled Risgan. "The tribespeople are cattle to you. The healing of the matron, the wellbeing of your brothers, all a sweet charade. You care only for your own interests."

"You make it sound so sordid!" Xoltux cackled. "'Tis only business, you know."

"Business, business, 'tis always about business. And the grief of the world for it."

"You are wise enough to voice it, but stupid enough to venture into this neck of the woods."

Risgan made a sad sound. "I thought to have lost my way, indeed. As too you and my enemies back on the river, whom I thought were engulfed in Nalsi's web."

"Bah! Those fools couldn't hit the broadside of a boulder."

Risgan hoped to keep the spirit-chaser talking. For he sensed that another menace was prowling nearby—a sacred owl or some brand of eerie fowl, perhaps even an ulsimar that might have snaked its way close to the sounds of voices. Feeling the prowling marauder skulking and pacing, Risgan knew that any threshold of escape might have already passed. The shaman had cornered him; now Xoltux waved his wretched magic stave in his direction.

Risgan recoiled as a strand of creeper vine edged down and caressed his shoulder with a sense of eeriness. Xoltux gave an explosive snigger, seeing the look of petrified horror on the relic hunter's face. "You can heal the dying, make them young again, but yet you are afraid of a few straggles of spider vine? Hah! Are you a weakling then? Here, what about this?" He flourished the stave and the vines seemed to recoil. The weapon, a fetish new to Risgan's eye, was a thing of elephant bone mantled with the skull of a basilmurk. The stave was much like Risgan's lost truncheon, minus the skull.

"Watch!" the shaman called. "The vines are barbed and deadly, to the novice. But to me?" He thrashed a sinister loop of punishment with the weapon; the living tendrils gave way to greater breadth with little shrieks and hisses.

"Here, vermin, feel the wrath of Xoltux!" he gloated.

Risgan leaped back with a grimace. He tried to follow the small path that was slowly arching shut in the trees, but too late. More tendrils had closed over the ivy in defence. It seemed as if the walls of vine were alive, like insects.

"Now—give me the jewel," croaked Xoltux icily.

Risgan hesitated. The shaman's eyes gleamed with a malignant fury.

Visions of power swam in his zealot's orbs. A discord stewed there—of power and ambition, warring with fear, and the neediness for complete adoration of his peers.

Risgan seeing the burning fervour in those eyes, reached in his pouch. He saw no profit in keeping the bauble in his possession and he tossed the charm to the ground, unafraid of the consequences.

"Very good," said Xoltux, nodding. "Now explain how it works." He prodded the relic with his stave, fearful to touch the thing himself.

"One side offers youth, the other, death."

"That's too ambiguous. Which one?" the shaman shrieked. "Which one offers death?"

Now it was Risgan's turn to bare his teeth with peevish anger. "Why should I tell you? You're a loathsome snake, an opportunist, a backbiter and a blackguard. You'll only use it for depraved ends."

The shaman gave an uproarious caw. "And who are you to pretend to use the magic for pure and altruistic means? Some healing avatar?" He snorted. "I'll tell you why you will give me the information, Outlander. Because if you don't..." He rapped his formidable staff on the turf. Tumultuous sounds entered the glade, like whining hornets or locusts. "Tell me now! Or do you wish to suffer extreme repercussions?"

Risgan returned a lackadaisical smile.

"Then die," sighed the shaman. He swung the stave in an arrogant loop calculated to inflict maximum pain upon Risgan.

The relic hunter backed away. He peered left and right. Dismay flooded his heart. A terrible roar had pierced the stillness. Now the long patch of quicksand which had blocked the way, gurgled and glooped in a terrible fury. In fact, a large gibbeth had made a sudden leap, attracted by the angry shouts, but had miscalculated and tumbled into the mire. Now the creature was struggling for its life in a suction of unrelenting forces. The shaman laughed. The ugly head was only a turquoise-matted thatch visible above the straining muck.

"You thought to gull me into carelessness, did you, Outlander? What, and fall prey to this foolhardy gibbeth? Ha! I am too quick for that." He croaked. "I've known it's been stalking us for a while now. Nevertheless, a brave sally on your part, considering the creature could have as easily devoured you as me."

Risgan crouched and reached out a trembling hand for the relic. The shaman did not interfere; the bauble lay shining in sinister view at his feet in the limp grass.

Xoltux ogled the coruscations on its edges with hungry anticipation. He screeched orders at Risgan to relinquish its mysteries. It was then that another creature struck without warning.

The youth talisman went flying, rolling under the thunder of powerful, webbed feet.

The kodo, a creature more comfortable on four legs than two, stood staring at Xoltux with large saucer-shaped eyes burning. The creature was some gruesome breed of hairless ape, peculiar to the semi-tropical forests. Its stiff quills like a porcupine's radiated from scalp to shoulders. The creature boasted a baboon's crouch, large powerful limbs and a flexible tongue that shot out twenty yards, as it did now, to curl around the shaman's waist, with just enough coiling gummy loops of strangling strength to prompt from the zealot a frightful gasp.

Xoltux seemed struck senseless. But he was not completely powerless. He had managed to blurt out a fragment of a spell and rap his stave twice on the turf before he was completely enveloped.

The kodo was pitched sideways in the magic's wrath. A freak tug of wind, or some malevolent waft, forced the creature slipping into the mud, dragging the shaman with it, who was wrapped in its filthy tongue.

Risgan did not linger to witness the grisly scene. There were sick howls of madness and flurries of thrashing that offended his ears.

He snatched up the talisman and fled without a moment's thought. He crashed through the vines, squeezing past sap-oozing trunks. Over a huge rotten stump he staggered and mossy stones. Never had he run so fast. Where there was one kodo there would be another, so Risgan justified his unseemly flight. There was some ghoulish quirk of justice here—Xoltux falling to the kodo, though the retriever did not care to analyze it. No more did he think of the shaman, only he pondered his own escape and the undeniable fact that the relic was cursed. An enigmatic bonding had linked him and the gem together, and it seemed he was destined to carry it...

2: The Mantaray coast

Risgan did not realize how close he was to the estuary of the river Vlon and the sea. The water glinted through the trees and he came out of the wilds a haunted man, bedevilled by gibbeths, usilmars, basilmurks, wet worms, leeches, wire snakes and other such creatures.

At his wits' end he had one murky night clawed his way up a giant mandrake tree to elude the coiling tongue of a kodo—long ago he had lost his famous purple powder renowned for deterring gibbeths, though he doubted if such preventative would actually gain any protection against a kodo. No sooner had he escaped the creature than he was set upon by several large grey flapping things—perhaps Nalsi's legendary stone owls. Shouts and frantic knife hacks had repelled the brood at last, though gnashing beaks and talons had ripped his clothing and drawn blood.

The trees finally broke, and the river, to his left, became a wide sluggish bay, almost a lake. Vaster than vast, the sea still ranged east and west, but of colour much more muted aquamarine. He prayed to Douran that shelter would find him here, for he was spent.

A family took him in, for he had stumbled the last few steps to their fishing village three leagues from Fugis. Upon seeing his emaciated and haggard condition, the wharf-side fishermen gathered him up and gave him food and shelter for the night. Risgan had no coins to offer, save three measly curios hidden in his pouch, which they refused, professing that he could repay them by joining their fishing crew with Alred and his son Albrek. Every morning they went out every to troll for gizza.

Within a week, Risgan had healed himself of his wounds to tolerable shape, though he hosted new scars and bleak memories of the perilous flight through Mangor forest. Though he should have been the worst for it, he appeared to have recovered much of his vigour, much to the amazement of his hosts. They saw a half dead man arrive, and within days an energetic figure rise from the ashes, looking even younger than when he had come. In truth, Risgan did feel more spry; he looked a few years junior than when he had left Xoltux wrapped in the kodo's tongue. Wryly he reminisced that the youth talisman's magic had healed Varwa as easily as him, for it was during the handling of the nephrite during his showdown with the shaman, that the miracle had taken place.

A league out to sea, Risgan assessed his duties on the *Drifting Sparrow*, meandering in the drowsy heat, rocked by lazy swells. It was a mid-sized scow powered by a single sail, square-cut, equipped with foredeck, twin companionways, aft deck, fore cabin and a clever telescope which swivelled on a pedestal by the ship's wheel. Nets were hauled onto the deck, assisted by Alred and his winch while his son manned the wheel. Risgan was relegated to sifting fish, bagging 'Aukwoks', 'Ters' or 'Gizza', which were consigned to the oily drums as and when necessary. Stoically, he accepted his fate, though he felt he could be doing better things, none worse than sitting in a gibbeth's belly. The ritual lasted for a few fortnights, and Risgan gained muscles he never knew he had. He bore the sun-tanned look of a rugged sailor who had seen many moons of service. The *Drifting Sparrow* became Risgan's temple and before long he grew attached to the hulk, accustomed to the rhythms, quirks, creaks, and shifts and sighs of the sea-battered scow. But the vessel had the unpleasant luck of being set upon by corsairs shortly after a morning's haul when the gulls were swooping and crying for remains of fish. The battle had been brief; none too elegant, and Risgan was only spared his life, courtesy of his quick tongue and clever wit which seized the moment and sized up the dozen ruffians springing down on the deck, armed with sharp sabres and gizza hooks. Alred and his kin were cut down before a word had been spoken. Risgan mourned their loss, but realized there was nothing he could have done. After dispatching of their bodies, the pirates hauled their fish onto the decks of their own craft, a square-rigged, twin-masted barque, and a few other items of wealth. The captain and his mates examined Risgan with some saturnine regard.

"Well then, varlet, who are you, and what's your story? Are you as quixotic as your dull friends who have died? They perished in vain—guarding this vessel and hoarding a few heads of fish."

"They did," cried Risgan, rising with zeal. "Know it your days are numbered. This vessel is protected by powerful spells!—Douran's, Fevis's and Fentlemeist's. Marsimor, a magician feared amongst the Mage's community, has enacted a malediction. His circle boasts high repute in these parts. Look carefully! I possess this seal—" he held up the Fuzuli curio "—an ornament passed from the mage to my own person—a rune of horror and vengeance!—one which will wreak woe on your miserable hides." He held high the talisman. "See now and be afraid!" The relic gleamed with a black and red-edged light in the sun's glare. It was the same given by Nalsi, which was mounted on a primitive runestone, the same he had been saving for just such an untoward occasion.

The superstitious pirates grimaced and stepped back, crowding around each other, feeling the same clutch of doubt and awe. A raucous laugh broke out as one spoke:

"This is nothing more than one of 'em pygmy-fetishes, Cap'n. Listen—we have here a funny little jester in need of a bloodletting."

"Aye, don't kill 'em too quickly, Cap'n! The blighter's got h'self a quick clever mouth. Quick-tongued, if I've 'eard one before. 'E's got h'self another yarn to tell us, I believe."

Risgan put on a show of indignant disapproval. "Your low-caste talk strikes no terror in me."

"Aye, nine lives this 'ere one's got," cried another. Three teeth stuck out his black maw. The bandit advanced, waving a scimitar, black bandanna wrapped about his balding head, showing dragons and the slit moons of the pirate brotherhood, which fluttered in the breeze. "Let 'im speak. He's got another tale afore we sail and send 'im to Hades' Hole!"

"Quiet, rogues!" advised the captain rudely, pushing his mates out of the way. He raised palms. "I'm sure this gentleman has more amusing tales to share, should we squeeze them from him."

The dialect of these thugs would have amused Risgan any other time, except now when numerous gullet-swabbing blades swarmed about his neck—clutched in the hands of roguish cretins who had so bloodily disposed of his friends.

"Aye, a whole lot more yarns, I've got," Risgan said growlingly. He thought to play the cutthroats against each other—if only to gain himself a few moments more of life. "If you survive Marsimor's magic, which at least heralds the spell of the distended brain, then you'll wish you were less crass in your jests!"

"Aye, we've ears for jests, varlet! Keep 'em coming. Tell us more of this Marsimor yarn."

"Where are you fine men heading?" Risgan stalled. "Certainly not out for a fishing excursion?"

"What's it to you, boy?—and that ain't a yarn. I think you're heading for a wee walk on the plank, if you don't wizen up. Keep 'em stories coming. How old 'er you anyway? A few days past puberty?"

Risgan petulantly forwarded an assertion that he was not a day less than forty five.

Wild roars erupted from the crowd. "See how funny 'e is?"

"Never mind," barked the captain. "This lubber seems to have a bit of nerve." The captain seemed a lot brighter than his doltish henchmen, without the annoying dialect that Risgan found hurtful to his ears. "We head to Snaggler's Point, just off Windman's Bay. We seek the lost ship of *Vistes the Valiant*. Once a year his ghost ship rides, so the legend says in the fog of pale magic blue. The caravel's fat with all her spoils the day she sank! Ripe for the picking, so we means to get her and carve us up a merry portion of her treasure!"

"An admirable expedition!" commended Risgan.

"Ain't that the truth?" echoed the captain.

Jester, the captain's mate, a small, blunt-nosed, sneaky brute, made a jocular comment which stirred the rogues. "Captain Karshan says we is looking for a few stout mates, we is—to accompany us on this here voyage and share the spoils with fearless reavers and adventurers in which we number few."

Risgan did not like the looks of this dirty oaf, nor the treachery etched in the eyes of his misfit mates. He demurred and put on a thoughtful expression. "Ordinarily, I might put in for such a post, Sir Rogue, being a blithe sort, but sword-fighting and hackwork are not my style of late. A bout of over-adventuring in Mangor Wood has made me dulled of late. I am too old for this roguery, withal."

"Too old?" The declaration spawned wild laughs and the captain muttered a biting oath. "We could leave you on Deadman's Isle, then—'tis a few leagues out to port. The shark infested waters there are no joy—but I hear a few men have lasted up to thirty days on that isle on coconuts and caterpillars, that is, before the cannibals stormed in on war canoes to hunt them down with their poison arrows."

Risgan's hand fluttered nervously to his throat. "In this case I must accept the challenge of boatswain, which would be sheer folly on my part to bypass."

"A sensible plan," muttered the captain. "Then let us to it." Beaming broadly, he bawled, "Ivith! Harvix! Welcome our new rogue to our clan."

There were hisses and cheers, some less exuberant than others. Risgan made mental note of the lukewarm exclamations and managed to amble his way without persecution about the midship deck. On high flew the red, black and yellow banner of *Yaster's Revenge*. So the barque was named, and Risgan was spared his hide—for now, at least.

The pirates put to anchor and rowed longboats to the next port of Willdown where they sold their choicest wares. They whored and gambled, and took off to sea again, keeping their wits about them, also tight watch on the newcomer, so that Risgan could hardly have chance to give them the slip, or tell the law of their secrets, or where they put to port, or their numbers, or their plans or their covert hideouts along the rugged coast.

The grisly work of the pirates went on: slayings, ship burnings, deck-fighting. The creaking hold grew plump with plunder: furs, fish, metals, fruit, fabrics and slaves until Risgan could stand it no longer. He felt he had absorbed so much death and misery and treachery and deceit that he had earned the malevolence of more gods than he cared for. He had taken care not to participate, nonetheless, in any of the slayings.

The ship lay anchored at four fathoms and they rowed the rest of the way in to Kavilstack, two leagues up the coast to celebrate their conquests at the *Bouncing Brothel* Inn. The mates set into a bit of festivities after a week of fruitful plundering. There were women, grogs, and beer and wine by the keg. The ship rocked gently in the moonlit swells at harbour, with only the unlucky Cuckstau the lookout, to guard.

The sailors knew the port well, for they had selected a few familiar fancies, who they cozied up to in the dim confines. A vile smoke wreathed the blackened beams; knobbed posts hung with dripping oil and rushlights on brackets which burned a feeble glow. Porthole windows let in some of the thin moonlight and an evil smell wafted about, courtesy of the fish-fat-fed lamps. Women's laughter drifted from upstairs, riding the breaking of glass and numerous other untoward sounds.

Rounded about the table were Karshan and five rogues of his crew and Risgan, drinking rum and talking the exaggerated talk of all sea dogs. When Risgan asked the reasons why he was still muzzled and kept like a pet, the captain answered in a few laughing words: "The world is too full of sly scoundrels like yourself, rogue. I lie awake wondering how you coaxed your way aboard my vessel and yet remain still alive."

Ambrose the navigator loosed a guffaw. "If you lie awake dreaming of this lank-limbed lubber, Cap'n, then there's no hope for you."

Karshan drew back and reached out a knobbed fist to grant Ambrose a stiff smack on the nose. Risgan was offended by the crassness with which he was forced to keep company. He mustered a frown. "You suspect that I'll desert your noble band and quest, after all you have provided me? What do you take me for, an ingrate?"

The captain curled lips in a good-hearted, but evil smile. "That and more. You just would not believe the number of tricky little rascals I've seen in my day, the bulk whom I've had to put to the sword."

Risgan laughed huskily. "You'll have no fear of that. Watch as I win you more wealth than you have ever seen. More than any on that mangy little fur freighter of yours." He sized up the first adjoining game of Sea-Blackey, and inserted himself easily into the game. Secretly he had been studying the bids for some time now, and noticed several small flaws in certain players' styles.

With a practiced hand, Risgan inserted some of his own cubes into the fast-flowing game. These he had stolen the previous night from the *Mariner's Inn's* tables and managed to modify them with dye, knife and scraper in the limited minutes of his own privacy. Risgan felt the gambling lust come over him—it was fuelled by a strong instinct to survive, which he deemed a good sign.

Risgan's continued winnings created a stir amongst the villains, and light camaraderie progressed to muttered curses.

"Here, you! You seem to be quite fluent with this Sea-Blackey game," grumbled Karshan hotly. "Darsh here, the undercook, looks ready to slit your throat, if you take any more of his gold."

Risgan did not doubt it, and he feigned innocent surprise at the size of his winnings. Snarls of agreement filled the air as he involuntarily touched his purse of mounting gold.

"How be a quick rub up with our favourite, Nauselia?" grunted the captain. "You've enough funds. I'll safeguard your valuables for you in the meantime."

"Admittedly, an attractive idea," murmured Risgan. "But I'll leave you to your fancies, Captain. I'm a married man and I would not think of upsetting my vows."

"Is that a fact?" Jester crowed, nearly in tears. "You? Married? You're just a baby!"

Ivith the crow's-nest man cried out a mirthful jest. "Here lads, 'tis another good gag from our Rizgany dear—we shall have laughs for moons to come."

Risgan gritted his teeth. The thought of spending month on month with these loons was insufferable. Not to mention they thought nothing more of him than an unblooded waif. He was just biding his time, looking for a ripe chance to make a break from their uncouth company anyway.

Oddly enough, the time was now. Ivith had just slipped upstairs for a round with Nauselia and her buxom, round-bottomed mate. Meanwhile, the captain was having a good time at Sea-Blackey, slated next on Nauselia's list, laughing raucously over his frothing grog and a bawdy joke or two traded by the innkeeper and the grim cook Fark. Fesalie and Korge were just warming up to a game of 'Yip-Yob' with a crew of local fishermen, a sport involving a heavy metal thong whirled on the end of a stout wire, that was to be caught barehanded by any stalwart or lionheart who dared it.

Leaving his stash, Risgan slipped out the back way unnoticed. He was on his way down the seaside path when a dog snarled. He stopped short, expecting fangs to come chomping into his leg. But they were not for him. He continued on, sidling like a weasel, attempting to make as much distance from the rogues as possible. The ocean was a blanket of stillness to his left, shimmering with moonlit rivulets of amber and gold. The moon was high in the sky and the air a muggy wash. Broken shells and crushed stone were slick with dew collected in the wee hours.

Risgan, gloating at his vanishing act, reminisced over what a bunch of fools these drunken hooligans were, and he congratulated himself on his easy escape.

He half-ran and half-jogged for the last few leagues, until, unable to plod on, he banged on the barnacled door of the *Mariner's Keel* Pub at the sea wharf 'Thistly'. Fortunately, he had a few coins tucked in his boot which he could offer the landlord—a surly fellow, who poked his nose out and gave him a curse, but accepted the two gold florins Risgan thrust into his palm.

Risgan lay down to sleep in the back of a rude storage room, enjoying the sleep of the dead, sniggering to himself on his timely luck.

Cockcrow came early and Risgan was not amused when Jester came busting into his cubbyhole early the next morning.

"Get up, you hog!" He and Ivith hoofed him awake and shook his limp body. His teeth rattled like a scarecrow. "What do you think of deserting us? We had a pact."

Risgan wiped his bleary eyes. "We did, and I was only out for a little jog. Heavens to Betsy! I must have dropped in fatigue before being taken in by the kindly landlord."

"Is that a fact?"

"'Tis."

"And three leagues away?" inquired Ivith.

"Is it that far?" Risgan gasped in surprise. "I must have lost track of time. By Douran! It pays to be fit on a sailing ship and I should be commended for my industry."

Jester and Ivith blackened both Risgan's eyes, despite his putting up a good fight and they hailed the punishment as a 'future lesson' should he try anything as fancy. The two bullies dragged him to the longboat beached on the sand nearby, and onto the barque which lay anchored within sight out ominously in the harbour.

The captain examined the roughed-over body of Risgan. "A delay. Two days and a night we must be at Snaggler's Point. Do not incommode us again." He turned on his heel and marched to the midship deck where he bawled orders to his mates. The sails were unfurled. The fast runner made way, north by west.

Risgan felt himself in another dream...

Some of the sailors were less keen than Karshan to undertake the mission, so far northwest up the Mantaray coast. It seemed that dire legends lurked in many a mind about a certain 'Kraul', and 'Seaworm' and other names like 'Vorcifer'. Mutters and sullen whispers were traded and revealed such titles as sea monsters of evil repute.

Risgan could hardly believe the yarn of an absurd 'blue fog' that would assail them in the expanse of cloudless sea.

"There will be fog, lubber—fog galore, just you wait!" sneered Ambrose, the navigator.

Risgan pushed his face out in a puzzled frown. "Why are we veering so far aft then?"

The old quartermaster gave a shrug. He waved a gnarled forefinger to the broken shoreline. "See those rocks? You don't want to pass by them too close. There are grottos in behind."

"So?" Risgan made an offhand gesture.

"They're the haunt of Grinneth, ye idgit. And you don't want to cross her."

"Grinneth?"

"A thing of shadow. Men don't know what she is, if a she, she be— none have seen the monster or survived to tell of her horrors, but just her breath makes all the sea monsters seem like puppets of sock and wool."

"Indeed," mused Risgan, finger to his mouth. "One would have never imagined such fearsome wights on your coastline."

The mariner gave a disdainful snort. "'Tis not *my* coastline, lubber, 'tis the coastline of the gods, to whom we all pay homage... " On that didactic note, others grumbled. "For the fools who have ventured inland to search for gold and treasure," claimed Ivith, "none have returned to spend a coin. They have all met *Grinneth*—and let us hope we do not either."

Risgan was not pleased with the information.

The horizon was flushed with the rose of coming dusk and the indigo sky dimmed a deeper shade. The ship anchored a half league out from shore where the black rocky cliffs rose with perhaps more menacing aspect than would be liked. Large shadow-ridden caves could be seen lurking with the naked eye. The old tarred timbers creaked with the effort of stalling in the sullen water. The peninsula to starboard made a long arm out to sea, now seen to Risgan and the sailors' eyes as a dull blur. Past Snaggler's Point skulked a hidden channel veering inland, so it was told, where the ghost ship of Vistes was reputed to ride on the 22nd day of Vilos, month of the Sea Dragon... *tomorrow*, Risgan discovered. The pirates would be waiting. Karshan gave orders to his men to curb their revelries for tonight. Come morn they would face brisk trials.

The first glow of dawn came early. Muted glimmers fought through a thick mist. Sure enough, there came a blue fog. A wall of mist, rolling in dense billows. Only by memory could the mariners navigate the treacherous stretch of coastline.

The ship limped through the thick swirls, more sluggish than ever. It was as if her barnacled hull were ever pulled back by invisible strings. Karshan thought this odd and cursed the ship's slow progress. The lethargy of it was an ill omen. Some old sea-sense of the captain's felt the first tremors of catastrophe, and the seaman drew a sharp intake of breath. All the sailors felt it, that and a sinking dread, and it was not helped by the captain's quirky way of fretting with his golden beard.

"Look lively, girls. Hostas! Jerl!" Karshan chided. "Clew up those sails. Trim the sheets. Lay wide the yardarms. We are not here to gossip on some joy ride!"

The pirate ship limped on; the preternatural silence grew. The still water seemed suspended in limbo for an eternal instant. Then there came a rush; the wild cascade of waves erupting in full force around them.

Huge claw fingers thrust up around them, with parallel pincers arching around the hull, imprisoning the midship. It was Kraul—sea monster and crab! Large enough to fill a ship, large as their ship and more, with her square sails and her fifty feet of proud length. Kraul's twenty pincers had them pinched unquestionably...

Timbers cracked. Hull planks split. The crab below was their master, with a shell hard and white and a pink carapace lifting the keel.

Arold the ship's carpenter, maintained a quixotic pose and hewed mercilessly at a reaching pincer. The claw jerked instantly and casually plucked him aloft with sword and sea hooks and therein threw him past the bowsprit out to sea where a horrid head reached up and snapped out with crunching jaws.

Risgan stepped aside in croaking dismay. The crab's head was green. Red bifurcated horns protruded from its hideously fanned skull, a chitinous curve, while blue eyes rolled on stalks and peered out with malevolent curiosity.

The ghost ship of Vistes rode alongside the doomed barque. Through the thick fog it sliced, a sail-less, skeletal wreck. Her bow plaque showed the name 'Vassal' and she passed them by with effortless ease, unhindered by the sea crab or any other menace, no farther than thirty yards off to *Yaster's Revenge* side. The skeletons on the deck peered over the rail, waving cutlasses and yelling warnings and uttering jeers. Karshan's men screamed in response and their wails became gurgling cries of terror as the crab dove slightly underwater and water flooded the bilges and the foredeck and poured in at her seams. Risgan dodged the cracking masthead and was instantly thrown out between a pair of pincers into the chill water. Others were not so lucky. They were snatched up in thick, hard claws and thrown into its pike-toothed maw. Risgan did not pause to examine the carnage. He flinched as the sound of splintered skulls and snapping bones became grisly crunches in his ears.

Other mariners dogpaddled along with him, with no less vigour than his own—Jester and Karshan—two souls who had escaped the wrath of Kraul. More followed—Jakus, Ivith, Minc and Vivefon. Of the thirty some pirates, only six had escaped.

"Quick!" gasped Karshan, choking on a mouthful of sea water. "Make for shore! 'Tis less than a half league."

"But Grinneth... she rides," jabbered Jester.

"Curse Grinneth! I'll take Grinneth over this shell horror any day!"

Risgan saw the logic. The splinters and mayhem and cracks and roars and splitting timbers raged behind.

The seaman Vivefon was terrified of the legend enough to swallow a lungful of water and drown. Jakus, upon witnessing this omen in the form of his death, dogpaddled away from the slaughter of Kraul and out to sea—Minc took his lead. Karshan shook his head in contempt. "Fools!"

Magically, the mist had lifted. With new hope, the fugitives scrabbled toward the shore of the bleak peninsula of land.

It was not surprising that the sailors were fearful of such caves as those that dwelled here. Risgan guessed they were jagged mouths of pure black volcanic rock at one time as he bobbed wretchedly in the swells. The wind struck and waves crashed against the rocks and shot up white foam. It was a death trap for ships, and likewise hapless mariners who had the bad luck of being forced to swim there. An odd way to die, reflected Risgan.

A bizarre, malformed isle drifted out in the foam a few bowshots away, nothing more than a bleak mound of basalt—with shale plates and stunted trees on its shores. Karshan identified the mass as Vishfike's Isle. Small solace they would find there, he moaned, starving and going raving mad. So, they swam to the mainland.

Karshan splashed a hand toward a less menacing passage amongst the rocks: a foaming green-black aisle of seawater. He had experience with ship wrecks before. With desperate strokes, they all pawed their way toward the gap.

It came as no astounding surprise that men told stories of mishap and bleak terrors dwelling in these straits. Sitting on three isolated rocks, poised three tall frog-like creatures with staring eyes. Yet with bodies like mermaids, at least a stone's throw away. Closer inspection proved the three to be frog-faced women, with feminine curves and fish fins. Dozens of white sticks crowded the slabs on which they sat, a further puzzle, marvelled Risgan. The creatures made no moves to intercept them. They only sat and stared at them like owls. Perhaps they were statues, put up by Grinneth or some other horror. To scare away explorers? Either way, none wanted to pass too closely to those sinister figures—except Ivith, who seemed exceptionally captivated by one particular faery and swam two yards nearer, ogling the nearest with a peculiar green glow and crude ridged brow.

The creature seemed fair to his eye; a long arm suddenly lifted him approvingly up to sit snugly aside her. They watched in frozen horror as

Ivith, smiling, still under the spell, seemed to enjoy his perch for a brief period, now looking like a small doll aside the admirer which in its proper perspective was twice the size of a man.

But as if awakened, the sailor grew fractious and thrashed blindly, trying to dislodge himself from his seat by the frog-goblin. The mermaid held him fast. Now it became clear the source of the bleached bones littering the rocks and with ever more industry, the survivors flailed away with the liveliest desire to escape.

The shellfish monster raged sullenly behind them, devouring the ship and its crew, crushing anything to bits in its path. Any men who happened to be still trapped there, perished in anguish. Finally the vessel sank, or was dragged under by the creature's claws, and there was silence.

The beleaguered mariners wallowed the rest of the way to the rocky shore. Into view came a tract of shallow water, somewhat sheltered from the incoming waves, and they stood waist deep in water, flush to the soaring cliffs. Left or right loomed sheer rock, vaulting up to staggering heights. There was nowhere to go. Ahead appeared only the shadow of a dim cave, with fangs of volcanic rock dripping from its crusty upper lip.

Jester whined; he blubbered on about the abominable deeds of Grinneth, purported to haunt the Point. Karshan silenced him with a buffet. Of what shape or terror the creature or ghoul was, neither seamen could say, for like the erstwhile quartermaster, they claimed none had survived to tell of the tale of Grinneth. Indeed, that it was only some mysterious entity which had claimed untold lives and demanded heavy tolls. Again, Risgan doubted this legend, but did not offer objection. In light of current grisly events such would imply denial. His mind rounded on a curious thought: it was said that the gibbeths came from caves near the sea, he recalled—once swimmers and water dwellers themselves, perhaps half-fish. Were gibbeths perhaps some offspring of Grinneth?

Risgan chuckled at the foolish extrapolation. He was becoming ridiculously imaginative. He paddled apprehensively into the cave with the others, wading into an enormous cavern. Pale light leaked from the cave's entrance, to illuminate the features of the grotto in an eerie golden-green sheen.

Almost motionless, the water stretched as far as could be seen. Small ripples lapped gently on the porous rocks to either side, with the ceiling fanned out high to great heights. From the cave mouth drifted the distant sound of crashing waves.

The intruders gained a patch of dry shore to their right flank where a belly of arched ribs stretched out for many yards—a huge whale's skeleton, if Risgan knew better.

Deeper they crept into the gloom, longing for a means to rise to the surface and escape this oppressive grotto. None relished the prospect of turning back, facing the horror of Kraul, should the crab remain.

With eyes adjusting to the darkness, the three castaways discovered a gargantuan ship, tilted on its side, preserved in time. The craft wallowed forlornly in the shallow water and slight mournful creaks issued from her hull. It was a ghost caravel, a three-master, whose tattered black sails hung in shreds and whose rigging was nothing more than creepers of broken, twisted cord. The hulk rolled gently in unseen currents. A jagged hole flew in her port strakes while water licked at her barnacled timbers.

Karshan waded in to inspect the antique lettering on the port side. "Vassal" is what he read.

"So..." he mused idly, "here lies the real Vistes' wreck."

"No ghost ship after all then?" asked Jester in wonder.

"There are doubtlessly diverse opinions on the subject."

"Then what was it we saw when the crab Kraul attacked?"

"Exactly what you said, a ghost ship—the ghost of the *Vassal*."

"How did it get here then?" demanded Risgan sullenly.

The captain leered. "Grinneth?"

"No treasure then?" spoke Jester.

"None." With hollow eyes, the party waded past the wreck and each thought the same thing: how had the caravel found its way into this cave? The narrow gap through which they had come was too small to fit it. There must be other exits and entries in this complex.

The uneven shore took on an unearthly hue as the three embarked on an upward climb on a somewhat torturous path. The pool sank below in black-green shadow. The natural light dimmed; before long they were lost in near darkness. The team scrabbled around on their hands and knees; desperately they prodded in the darkness like blind old beggars. Each felt his own private terror: three lost men, doomed, bedraggled birds in a mysterious cage. Soon they began to hear voices—hums, laughs, titters. It caused Risgan grim shudders. It could have been the voices of deceased mariners, or the chatter of mischievous mermaids, but 'twas neither. All could only assume it was Grinneth.

Presently they heard a rush of water—a welcome sound, then they caught sight of a small triangle of light etched in the rocky ceiling a stumble and jog away.

Their hopes flared. The trio dashed toward the patch of luminescence, but no sooner had they reached it, when their feet dropped out from under them. It was a false floor set in the stone, down which they slipped in the current of a black chute of water.

Blackness overtook them. Had the snare purposely been laid? Risgan had no answer. Many feet they plummeted. How many, the mismatched comrades could not say, only that they splashed down into another body of water, large and mysterious, still and dank. There they heard the fated echoes of their splashing as if they were in a limitless cavern. Into another grotto they had plunged—much larger than the last.

The seamen peered at each other with hooded eyes. Daunting stalactites dangled down from an invisible ceiling. Like giants' claws they loomed. They treaded water in depths much over their head. A dim glow burned from somewhere, afforded by skyholes—in some ceiling of fantasy? To their relief they saw a weave of sunlight knitted off to the side, somewhere beyond the pool where they had heard the crash of waves.

A cave mouth! Risgan gasped. It was a matter of simplicity then! All they needed to do was swim to the open water and out of the reach of the sea monster lurking somewhere on the other side of the tongue of rock.

But there came an odd splashing from that direction and then the sound magnified. The men floated in mute trepidation, hardly daring to move their arms to keep them afloat.

They squinted in the dimness. They could see a flutter of fibrils, hanging silver, vermilion, taupe, from some dim place across the channel on the far, rock-cave wall. A grievous voice filled the echoing chamber: old, creaky, dreadful...

"Welcome, mariners! Do not fret. You'll be well taken care of. Please be at ease! You reside in the atrium-salon of Grinneth."

Risgan blanched. To search for the source of the voice was impossible; he could find none—only dripping water and foul drafts. A dimly sparkling net of silver and carmine threads continued to shine from the cave where a cool, musky wind blew, possibly the breath of Grinneth.

The waves crashed beyond on the rocks that gleamed with sunlight... so far away, and yet so temptingly near, but with a foreboding of dread and doom.

"I see you have found my lair," came the tortured voice again. "Few visitors do. Usually I have to force myself to net my guests. Ha! With Kraul and Vorcifer fighting over my spoils, I grow weary of strife and competitiveness. Of late, I have secluded myself in my lair. A convenient enclave! One day I will deal with the avarice of Kraul and the others. 'Tis unimportant! My mermaid minions are slack these days; sitting idly on their rocks. They blink languidly and make limp gestures that only fools would heed and venture so close as to be snatched up. Well, my vassals and I feasted plenty for long years and cannot complain."

There was a long pause, and Karshan, sensing the need for words, spoke in a voice dread and devoid of pretence. "Ivith has satisfied your hunger and at this moment sits aside one of your frog-women. There is no point to repeat the exercise on us. I believe the offering suffices as adequate tariff for passage and that we should remain unmolested."

The deep voice laughed languorously. "The logic is ill, wayfarer. It creates a stress on my ear. Behold my champion, Gorgere!" A strange wind blew toward an area of the pool where splashing ripples suddenly broke the surface. An indistinct head bobbed up. "Gorgere is a staunch vassal, a capable stewardess, wardress of this hall, if you will. She has been instructed to take 'tolls' and is quite good at it."

The three gazed bleakly at the creature that had surfaced in the dim light. Only a few yards away, bobbed a mermaidish hybrid of human and epiphod, obviously a protector and haunter of the place from the grotto to the open sea. Most of the mermaid's body was submerged; only the fair head showed with glistening russet hair and two wide-spaced green eyes from a fine, aristocratic face.

Risgan gave a bewildered gasp, for a sinuous fishy underbody wavered under that murky water. He squinted carefully trying to assess the malevolence of the aberration.

"Regard the cave," continued Grinneth sombrely. "These are no ordinary sights. The hanging stalactites are rare; they contain multiple stems and crystalline points almost cuneiform in shape. The stalagmites reside below the water and are sadly out of reach. This grotto was overwhelmingly flooded in the past aeon."

Risgan fashioned a knowing nod of scholarship while he tread water.

"'Twas one of the first things I noticed, Grinneth, and we are thankful for the information. Truth be told, I am low on coins, as likely are my peers, or gladly we would pay the toll. In retrospect, most sit on the bottom of the grotto for which Gorgere is free to plunge, as I'm sure her lung capacity far exceeds ours."

"Possibly so, but Gorgere is a moody creature and will doubtlessly reject such a menial task."

"I was going to express this very fact," remarked Risgan.

"The price for unsolicited entry into my hall is to bump heads with Gorgere. My, we shall enjoy the sport! As we always do. It has been an age since my champion has taken on three rogues. So, I shall delight, and so it shall continue, with all manner of mariners, fishermen and explorers for time immemorial."

Karshan and Jester uttered brief moans. Their bleary eyes swelled and chagrin dawned at the doom upon them. Risgan accepted the fact with an easy carelessness. His mind worked at furious speed. "So, who is to go first then?" he demanded. "I warn you, Grinneth, I am a stout fighting man and am better left till last."

The creature seemed to accept the claim. "And who will swim the chasm and win past Gorgere? The way is long, and the water is deep." The voice boomed from beyond the silver and vermilion flaps across the water.

The mermaid-creature Gorgere's piercing green eyes shafted upon Karshan. Grinneth seemed to sense the implicit picking and blew out an approving gust of wind from the cave to near freeze the captain's matted beard. "Well, Captain! It seems as if Gorgere has taken a fancy to you. Fate calls!"

Karshan bowed awkwardly in the water while treading water and chattering on with polite courtesy, "Mistress... Excellency. The honour is profound and too regal for my creaky bones and humble artifices. I nominate Jester, my mate, who has faithfully served me for eleven years and who is ripe for challenges of this nature."

Jester struggled in the water to quickly repudiate the suggestion. "The captain speaks hastily, Grinneth. Karshan is a maudlin sort, to boot. Too much of a gentleman—" he laughed "—and I wholly defer the exalted privilege to that gallant cavalier at my side to whom we have the honour of being in close company. His name is Risgan and he's a real life relic hunter."

The monster behind the dank veil blew a wash of nauseous air. Risgan's dripping curls fluttered. "What pleasure it is to be in the company of such august men! Well, Risgan? What of it?"

Risgan was left with a sour taste in his mouth at the gust and stared speechlessly at the creature. But then, he clapped his forehead in a sudden glum realization. "Another complication jars my mind. Gorgere speaks to me telepathically, whispering that the skinny newcomer Jester is to be first, as much as I hate declining first pick on the roster."

Grinneth seemed to pause in disbelief. Jester objected with all of the force of his soul.

Karshan likewise renounced the possibility of his following Jester in battle, an act which Risgan had helpfully suggested. There ensued a vicious squabbling amongst the three men and Karshan and Jester nearly drowned one other in the feud. Grinneth blew a fetid wind from the cave. "Silence! We must have peace. This tumult is unbecoming of knights of Grinneth's sports. Jester! You shall proceed first in the competition. I will brook no protests. Now at attention!"

Jester arrested his gibbering and glared fiercely at Karshan—no less, Risgan.

Karshan spoke with solemn reserve: "'Tis a great honour to precede us, Jester, as a man of your capacity should know. Stand pleased and proud."

Jester surveyed his mates with saturnine malice: "Must I bob and tread these chill waters listening to your drivel while I mentally prepare myself for the challenge of Grinneth's competition?"

"No," exclaimed Karshan, "but we are only forces of support and encouragement."

"Commence!" boomed Grinneth. "My ears tire of these banalities." The creature lifted the trap, or by some unseen force, a trigger mechanism slid back which caused a wide spray of floodwaters to fall flat from high places. Jester, farthest out in the water, seemed pulled along by the current, a deluge that became a roiling rapids. Risgan struggled to maintain his position and avoid being sucked out into the channel, likewise Karshan. "Ride the chute!" called Grinneth jocularly. Swept in the maelstrom of her pool, Jester scrabbled for the farthest shore closest to the rocks. A patch of light promised freedom. But the minion Gorgere was quick to act and easily caught him and played him like a flute, flipping him in the air like a silver salmon.

Jester cried out for help but was immediately pulled under by Gorgere.

Risgan winced. Karshan's eyes misted with concern. Jester came bobbing up again, green-faced, looking limp and exhausted. The face that showed next to his was that of a beautiful hybrid of mermaid and mermydion, with green emerald hair and glossy lips. The creature swayed sinuously in the water and scaly hips showed a gizza tail instead of legs. She opened her sensuous mouth; there were not pure white teeth, but fangs, and the creature hissed like a cat and Jester shrilled in protest. Arms or fishy appendages pulled him under and the mariner did not resurface.

"Next to come," intoned Grinneth, "is Captain Karshan. Gorgere has had her due, so we shall leave her for now; Captain, please... 'tis your turn."

Karshan gave a nervous snicker. "The contest is premature, Grinneth. I need time to collect my strategies."

"Do not mind Gorgere's frolic!" laughed Grinneth with raucous mirth. "She is a wise, spirited and feisty nymph, but never unfair, especially in the affairs of rogues. Likewise, she is sensitive to criticism, so I advise you to curb your pinched frowns. It disparages her. Look, I see ripples brewing. Gorgere arrives, and her eyes are sharp!"

Risgan and Karshan swiftly put on faces of affability and kindly forbearance.

Grinneth's voice took on a mellifluous tone. "I see you wonder of your peer's fate. In this, I feel I owe you an explanation... Of old, my ancestors, the star-wights of Kal-a-zar, collected men's spirits for the 'great lattice' as they coined it. One day it would be a complete verisimilitude of the avatar Fambar's life! A thousand, thousand weaves of grave bodiless souls! Strand after strand of emerald waterwork brimming with spiritual energy. The construction lies under the body of this inner lagoon. I rejoice in announcing that three more souls will soon join the lattice. Two, now that Jester is likely being sewn in the weave by Gorgere this very instant.

Karshan moaned and Grinneth signalled the completion of the weave with a blast of air that was disquieting. The creature motioned likewise to a glass tube positioned farther out in the water, pointing down in mysterious fashion, like some kind of ghastly telescope. The device was one foot in diameter and fused into the rock below. Karshan and Risgan swam over to peer down cautiously into the hidden, submerged depths of the grotto far below the bedrock. Skeletons were strung in that vast lattice, laced together in neat rows and patterns forming a fantastic mandala.

Risgan put finger to tongue and swallowed hard, for there was the pirate Jester now, eyes staring in abandon, hair waving in the water currents, precariously poised upon an unobtrusive edge of the 'weave'.

Risgan could hardly suppress an involuntary shriek. He looked to Karshan for hope. Karshan offered none. Risgan spun about in a loop of dull despair. What to do? "Wait, Grinneth!" he called. "If it is souls you seek, then let me offer this counsel. Several of Karshan's men, though deficient in intelligence, still live on Vishfike's Isle. 'Tis that bald wrack of rock not far from here. Isn't that right, Karshan?"

"'Tis true!" croaked the captain, grasping for any salvation as he wagged his head back and forth with pale-faced confusion.

"Even if all are dead, we can lure others to your lair," explained Risgan, "with whom you and your minion can deal as you wish. Your lattice can be engorged with mariners!... Think of it. Why settle for two mariners, when you can have a dozen?"

The captain corroborated the concept with an earnest appeal.

Grinneth hung on the words. She seemed intrigued with the concept and her meridian fibrils pulsed, hanging at the mouth of her cave. "Very well, vagabonds, we shall see to this, but I highly doubt that after aeons of luring men to my lair, you will teach me an innovation."

Risgan gave Grinneth an assured wave. "Never fear of that, Grinneth. You will be astounded. New innovations abound in my mind!"

"Of that we shall see." The wind blew ever cooler from Grinneth's cave. A luminous oval shape furtively parted the hanging threads to slip noiselessly into the pool. Risgan stared in morbid wonder. The creature, huge and hideous, swam next to them, an eerie, disquieting mass, beckoning the others follow to the end of the grotto where her grotesque hulk made ripples in the wan sunlight.

They waded out gratefully in the afternoon air, gratified to feel the yellow warmth of the sun. Grinneth's half-shimmering hump of a head and turtle's back brimmed above the waves and seemed to lose some of its ghastly sheen. The mainstay of her expanse undulated eerily underwater in the shape of some weird, mushroom-shaped goblin.

Jellyfish? Mollusc? Ctenophore? Risgan was at a loss to say. Karshan and he steered clear of the hundred luminous pink cilia that rippled like silky threads in the nearby waters. Gorgere thought to bring up the rear, veering in to nip at Karshan's heels should he flag.

The troupe swam to the island, which was several furlongs out. They steered clear of any frog-faced women that basked on the slabs. Grinneth's wake seemed to pave a smooth way amongst the rolling waves. There was no sign of *Yaster's Revenge*, Kraul or any other beasties, which was marginally encouraging.

The island loomed starkly ahead and they broached the broken shore of sea shells and grey-blue shale with fastidious caution. Before any could alight, Grinneth came alongside the company, pulsing in her malignant glory. Risgan thought to detect a vestigial face there, somewhat green and full of frightful teeth and glaring eyes beyond the comprehension of men in that slimy silver-crimson blanket of grisly evil in the shallow water, but they could not be sure. Gorgere was, for the nonce, confined to the water.

Risgan advised Grinneth: "In order to lure potential sailors, we must pass those caves on yonder ridge. Sadly, this is an inconvenience which must nullify both Gorgere's and your ability to accompany us. I know you are a creature of water, not land. This said, I suggest you stay here and bask in the waters and await for our speedy return with sailors from passing ships which must surely come within the next fortnight."

Grinneth composed what might have been a sullen grunt. "This comprises a small contingency, wayfarer. For it is said that Dag, the wood wight and troll, dwells in those caves yonder. But this should present no problem to men as hardy as yourselves. As a supervisory precaution though, I will consign Gorgere to accompany the captain on this journey, who believes, in light of common opinion about mermaids, that the mermydion can be no more agile on land as she is in water."

The captain framed a vehement protest to the claim but a monitory pulsation on Grinneth's head-stalk warned him to discretion, and he humbly conceded the honour of 'luring' to Risgan.

Grinneth made a pulsing snort of peevishness. "By no means! Risgan is fatigued from his swimming and must partake in considerable scouting. Presently he will be obliged to undergo a ritual, tasking to the spirit to which I have specifically assigned him in conjunction with the 'luring'. Needless to say, this honour is an act for which I wish him freshly alert."

"This is well and good but inconvenient to my plans!" the captain insisted crisply, but Gorgere rounded on him, and steered him back toward the shore. The captain planted feet reluctantly back on the loose blue shale.

As Grinneth had suggested, the epiphod Gorgere sprang out of the water, bouncing on her tail. Karshan, appalled by the action, swung his dripping body back with alarm. Doubtfully, he looked up toward the rugged ridge from which protruded a fan of stunted craybacks and slay bush. The Captain's attempt to creep back in the water was shunted by Gorgere.

"I should warn you," advised Grinneth, as she bobbed easily in the water, "that several will 'o wisps reputedly wander the crags. For such reason, someone is obliged to reconnoitre the thistle ways and scree that breast the caves. I do not care to tangle with Froth or the head spook, who makes Kraul look like a seraph of charity, thus, the task must devolve again upon the captain."

Karshan protested vehemently and stopped in his tracks. Ruefully, he professed to bypass the deed. "This is too much of a burden of merit—" at which Grinneth snapped a crisp command and the epiphod sank fangs into Karshan's arm and dragged him underwater. Karshan disappeared in a small whirlpool. There was a brief flurry of bubbles leading toward the grotto and Risgan assumed that the captain was hauled away to decorate Grinneth's 'weave'.

Risgan sighed in vexation.

Grinneth intoned: "I trust, Relic Hunter, that you are less assertive in your address?"

Risgan wagged his head and assured the creature that his intentions, while possibly unsophisticated, were of the strictest transparency.

"Good! This brings us to our next task! So then! To the caves! Captain Karshan's task is important."

Risgan, fearing the punishment of Grinneth, or rather Gorgere's punishment, disconsolately pulled himself out of the water and conducted himself with graceless speed upon the march upward. He thought of a thousand ploys which might rid him of the creature, but none seemed efficacious and Risgan gave up.

The relic hunter followed an old goat trail that wound its way up the ridge. Scree crumbled underfoot. A broken foundation of an old Masulurion keep nestled amongst the boulders and Risgan kicked at it. It blocked his path: a ring of square blocks in a tumbled heap. An even more desolate fang of rock rose in abandonment a furlong away—likely the haunt of Dag, if such creature existed. The sea stretched for endless leagues, with whitecaps rising like spring blossoms merging into the horizon. No trace remained of the mystical mist which had spawned the ghost ship *Vassal*.

For a long time Risgan wandered these gloomy heights, littered with cairns, stumps, wood beetles, skeins of twisted rock, and boulders. All the while Grinneth kept a brooding vigil below. He did not know how long he could keep up this charade, fearful to poke his nose in any cave, especially one that might contain Froth or Dag or some unimaginable horror gadding about the dark. He had no idea this coastline was so feral! What a misfortune! That he ever was waylaid by the dim-witted pirates of Karshan's creed weeks ago was certainly abominable!

Grinneth grew impatient with Risgan's laggardness and called up a sullen inquiry.

"Just so, Grinneth," answered Risgan, hands cupped about his lips. "I am searching for the proper place to pitch a small signal fire, even erect a temporary lighthouse with which I might signal numerous incoming ships. In fact, I happen to see a ship out to port, perhaps two leagues."

Grinneth harrumphed a note of triumph.

The mermydion Gorgere had returned from her macabre mission and under Grinneth's curt instruction, she slunk quietly out of the water to come springing up the slope on her fish tail, following Risgan up the lofty bluffs.

Risgan winced. Now his plans were under more pressure. From this distance the mermaid seemed indistinguishable from any of the frog-ghouls who sat idly on their perches in the wave-torn rocks not far away on the mainland shore.

Risgan increased the level of his industry. He searched, foraging with fervid haste, hoping for some object, clue, prop or advantage that might aid his plight. None presented themselves. He chanced upon a particularly loathsome sinkhole, a massive dark gopher burrow pitched between two basaltic boulders. It was dark and off-putting, between which emitted dank airs and a fetid reek. Bones hung in the periphery: of gulls, seabirds, auks, even a few human skulls, if Risgan weren't mistaken.

He recoiled. At that instant he was struck with a diabolical plan and the stench of unwashed hide made him almost lose consciousness. He saw a dim flutter of movement in the near darkness. What? The nearby orifice concealed something untoward. He paused, jerked sideways, made several tripping steps backward toward Gorgere, who happening to just arrive, hopped on her tail-fin, with a face frozen in an expression of stony displeasure.

Risgan cupped a hand about his lips. He urged Grinneth melodiously to revise her decree. "Look, fair Queen, fortune favours. Please mount the slope quickly! Gorgere has discovered a trove of men. They huddle in some dank cave, hiding from Kraul, or your net of terror."

"This is not surprising," called up Grinneth, "but the request is impossible."

"Why is that?" shouted back Risgan, ignoring Gorgere's insistent objections which seemed lost in the wind.

Grinneth wheezed an irate gust: "The act of climbing is inconvenient. Bring the men down to the waterside for me to examine. Waddling upon land in the open sun is intolerable to my disposition, insofar as I may fall vulnerable to foes who are less than my match in water."

"This is pure nonsense!" scoffed Risgan. "Your qualm is unfounded. Look, I tread on high near the caves unscathed and am but half your might."

The sea creature gave a snorting trill, but seemed not able to argue the fact.

Ponderously the sea wight raised her hideous bulk from the water and approached on all cilia with rare caution. The act was laborious and Risgan waited with nervous anticipation, despite Gorgere's obnoxious protests and hisses to the contrary.

"Where are all these men?" the creature at last cried, ignoring Gorgere as she pushed her way petulantly to the sinkhole.

"They are here, past this volcanic maze of boulders. You must surely see them after advancing several yards to the left. Carefully now! The stones are slippery. The men cower in disgrace."

The creature harrumphed and persistently shambled ten further feet, leaving a trail of grey slime behind her. There was a shuffle of movement, a sudden scrape, a plunge, and as a boot scuff came, a horrid guttural grunt followed. The Dag troll struck with deadly precision and Risgan bounded back with a brisk practicality. He sped past Gorgere whose fishy arms automatically reached for him, while he plunged pell-mell down toward the shore. There came a fierce scuffle, a thudding of blows as the troll, some juggernaut of impressive proportions, ripped hands into Grinneth's jellyfish body and pulled away great gobs of grey-green flesh. Grinneth, screaming in anguish, moaned. She expelled a heap of noxious vapours and fluids in the troll's face.

The effluvia momentarily blinded the troll. Risgan saw it was a hairy, horned man-beast, scaled and clad in shin and breast mail. The creature thrashed and kicked, bawling sounds not unlike a male gibbeth in heat. Risgan grimaced. He watched sombrely as Grinneth wrapped several slimy cilia about the troll's legs which seemed to paralyze the creature for an instant. The troll fell with a booming thud. Grinneth mounted him triumphantly, almost enveloping the reeking hide with her viscous slime. But the island troll was no simpleton to battles and he rippled his thews and gave a great roaring laugh. He had not survived these many decades for nothing. The demise was merely a ruse, a clever gambit to disarm the sea-fiend. Dag lifted himself with proud dignity and pulled the sickening sucking slimy body of Grinneth off his own and cast it contemptuously on the ground.

Risgan watched in spellbound horror as Gorgere attempted to hop forward to defend her mistress, sharp teeth sinking into the troll's forearm, but the troll simply laughed and gripped her thin waist in a mallet fist. The monster threw her far out in the water where she splashed and sank. There came bubbles and a lugubrious moan. Grinneth tried to slink away with what little remained of her motor functions, but the troll was livid, laughing and dragging her back into the sinkhole where he continued his pleasures. There ensued an interval of gnashing horror, terror-rich shrieks, moans of distress, thudding rocks, kicks, slashes, bites, blows, snarls, bellows, rage-filled sighs of fright and revulsion from which Risgan could make no differentiation.

For all intents and purposes, Grinneth was dead and Risgan gave a joyful cry. Gone now was the ghoul! He did a little jig and for not the first time did he congratulate himself on his victory. Though the members of *Yaster's Revenge* had faced Douran, he realized he alone had prevailed, as a result of his quick ingenuity.

He negotiated the dark waters back to the mainland, but a place far away from Grinneth's grotto. It was a swim he was grateful for, apart from the possibility of bumping into a lurking sea fiend, like Kraul or Gorgere, if such were alive. But of either no sign was seen. Likely the former was digesting his meal, and the latter had descended again, dead or alive, to that fabulous lattice so endearing to Grinneth, of which she was now its ultimate guardian.

2: THE TEMPLE OF VITUS

1: Borhoff

Risgan's plight was not a merry one as he struggled in the waters of the Mantaray Sea for yet the third time. Fortunately the tide was out and a northerly breeze pushed his body farther downwind the coast of Grinneth's grotto.

Risgan's lips were set in a grimace. He doubted much that his luck commanded much authority as he bobbed cork-like, thrashing at the water like an exhausted fish. The rocks reared dangerously ahead. After a time, aided by the rolling waves, he paddled his way to a sheltered lee of black sandy beach. He dragged himself onto the turf and lay there spent. A gentle surf licked his legs. Not far away another body lay sprawled—the unfortunate Minc's.

Risgan reeled back in surprise. A prickling dread pulsed through his body. He scuttled away with distaste; already crabs were gnawing at Minc's pocked features.

Masking his revulsion, Risgan debated whether to bury the corpse or go his way. He decided that lingering would be a waste of time; sea birds were already shrilling a signal of warning. Other creatures, less genial than Gorgere likely lurked about...

Risgan took to his heels. Several stones' throws away there sat the bedraggled form of the pirate Jakus, lounging on a flat rock, abreast the cliffs. He watched Risgan with cold wariness. His hair was a matt of spider-leg dreadlocks, the strands bleached dry after his own unquestionably tasking swim. The rogue's eyes were dark like spyholes into a murky world in a rough-tanned face. His body exuded a bitterness, a barely-contained hostility, plainly confirmed by his furled fists.

Risgan approached the pirate with casual good nature. He tipped his head in a friendly nod. "Hoy, Jakus, I see providence has called." He thrust a thumb back toward Minc's carcass. "I suppose we remain the only survivors of *Yaster's Revenge*."

"What of it? Where's Grinneth?" Jakus demanded harshly.

"Grinneth is dead."

The pirate shook his head with mulish disbelief.

"Don't believe it, do you?" said Risgan. "Grinneth is gone, mauled by a Dag troll."

"No such troll exists. Grinneth can never die."

"Believe what you want," muttered Risgan. He had disliked this seaman from the beginning. He cast a leery look back behind him to Vishfike's Isle, wondering if in fact, the creature Grinneth were dead. He swore he could hear the mournful voice of her crying out, and the roar of the death-dealing troll not far behind.

Risgan grimaced and Jakus drew closer while expressing a sardonic grunt. "And the others?—all dead?"

"I think that best describes their state. Best that we hightail it. This is an eerie locale. Nothing is to be gained by us mourning our plight and sitting around here trading long looks with the gulls."

Jakus only grumbled in indifference.

"So, where is the nearest settlement and shelter?" asked Risgan.

"Alvzar. Nothing but a goat heap, if I remember." Jakus's voice trailed off. "What's the point anyway? Soon we'll be prizes for the gibbeths—or other creatures which surely plague this bleak seashore."

"Cease your gloom," reproved Risgan. "I have not come this far to be hindered by a few creatures such as gibbeths. Are you forgetting that I faced Grinneth alone, and survived?"

Jakus grunted his disbelief and tossed his shaggy head.

Risgan did not like the way the pirate's eyes focussed on his dagger at his waistband. Jakus had no weapons. Likely the memory of his unlucky bout at Sea-Blackey back at the *Bouncing Brothel* inn was still fresh in the corsair's mind.

The two allies took company under an uneasy truce and negotiated the beach south. Boulders stretched down to the incoming surf and a few cypresses grew in dispirited stands. Risgan saw a dim headland showing itself in distant haze.

Conversation came in desultory waves. Neither man could care so much as to give an ounce of trust to the other.

Jakus did not suffer from the terrible low-caste dialect of his peers on Karshan's ship, to Risgan's thankful relief. The pirate, weaponless, attempted to bump casually into Risgan and pass a hand intimately close to his belt where the dagger was affixed. Risgan slapped the probing fingers away. "Hold tight! I am not a man who encourages intimacies." He brandished his weapon.

Jakus's lips peeled back in a smirk. His half circle of peg-like teeth glinted in the light. "I am suffering dizziness in this hot sun after a hard day's swim. Do you condemn me for that? Do not forget that I barely escaped the persecutions of Kraul myself."

Risgan mumbled out his pity. He put several paces between himself and Jakus; he was only mildly reassured when the pirate lengthened his stride and marched ahead. To forestall the effects of the pirate's wandering hands he kept his weapon bared.

The hours passed and if not for Risgan's foresight in securing a decent weapon and belt back in Bazuur, it would likely be himself scrounging for a poniard and Jakus grinning at him. Risgan congratulated himself on his keen forethought.

A better part of the day elapsed and the two walked the bleak shore for many miles. Each furlong disappeared in a dreamy haze and a tangle of rounded boulders. Only a few odd ships plied the Mantaray coast. These were weathered, broad-bellied fishing scows, tall three-masted merchant ships with unknown destinations. They gave the coast wide berth; invariably, all such ships were quite useless to them in terms of rescue.

The two had became infamously hungry and Risgan sought to try his luck at some gizza fishing. Jakus dismissed the idea out of hand. "You have no line. Best that we make much distance between ourselves and Grinneth."

"Grinneth, Grinneth, always Grinneth," Risgan chided. He threw up his hands. To convince this stubborn git that Grinneth was dead was an exercise in futility.

The beach widened. The cliffs somewhat dropped in height and shattered octagonal castles made themselves known on the craggy summits, casting knife-edge shadows down the seashore. The sun rounded its way westward. Waves crashed relentlessly on the shingle. Except for a few distant islands, the aquamarine blanket of sea seemed unblemished for leagues to come.

The bluffs continued to narrow and the two passed an abandoned seaside temple. Flush to the shore they spied shipwrecks—stout, bleached ribs of beaten timber lying askew, gleaming nakedly, with hulls plundered and seagulls floating about like white ghosts looking for the shades of mariners and unmourned spirits.

Risgan felt a gnawing despair. A crumbling old sea wall stood up ahead and farther up the beach, a jetty. Risgan's spirits rose slightly, for there loomed a framework of stone ramparts—perhaps an old village?

The relic hunter trained his eyes inland with excitement. Beyond the walls he saw pens and outbuildings looking much like stalls and stockades. The two trooped over to investigate, their curiosity wetted. Several animals in wooden cages began to take shape: lizards, fowl, hogs, teratyx, and other mismatched beasts imprisoned beyond whittled pales.

The cliff rose in behind the animal yard like a natural fence. At its summit stood a forbidding keep of breathtaking proportions. Closer to the shore, ranked stout wood-meshed cages containing various other animals. Similar cages dangled on cords slung from low to mid-sized rock towers. Rare birds such as sevix and memyews chirped behind the bars: strange salamanders, exotic sloths, hogs, pigeons and more—even a scrawny gibbeth roaming the perimeter of its cage, gazing out with feverish hope at the newcomers.

The surf crashed behind them, competing with the squawks, grunts and animal roars of the exotic menagerie. Woodcocks ran amok in the sand and Risgan thought to see a whisper of human movement...

Rubbing his eyes, Risgan wondered if he were in another dream. He half expected the time-smith of Fiffiholth to come whirling out of his emerald green tornado. But he did not, and the relic hunter gave a gasp of relief, for while realizing that this was no dream, neither was the foul breath of Jakus who strode impudently beside him.

Presently, they glimpsed the source of earlier indications: a large stocky man who stooped boldly before the base of one of the sturdy crayback-reinforced cages. An estimable kodo was trapped within—the pale grey tongue licked out from a face looking very morose. The man was middle-aged, and well muscled. Risgan saw that he was also missing an eye. Several scars showed on the fat pink of his bare legs. A caftan covered his upper body and he wore a pirate's orange bandanna. A short gleaming sword lay buckled at his waist. His one eye was bright and disarming, not dissimilar to those Risgan had seen on certain carrion birds or black ravens that came pecking about his dig sites looking for spoils.

The man caught sight of them and stood up in puzzled surprise. He was a half head taller than either of them and showed a face hardened by the years. "Well, what surprise does the Mantaray Sea offer today?"

"No surprise—just a pair of shipwrecked seafarers," remarked Risgan pleasantly. "We are looking for better fortunes than what lie up the coast."

"Is that a fact now?" the man chuckled. "I am Lubdar, an animal keeper and Lingarian trader—a zooman, actually. I am somewhat of a collector by nature."

"Sounds like an interesting hobby," remarked Jakus, sweeping a sunburnt hand to the scattering of cages and outbuildings.

"Not just a hobby," the other rumbled. "I sell these creatures to passing merchants—the highest bidders are the ones who get the merchandise."

He gestured a hand which missed a finger at the trapped kodo which looked morose with its drooping ears and clipped tongue. "Evil creature, old Ganvus is. I collect and rear animals of his type and sell them to specific buyers. See how the creature trembles in its own filth? A caravan comes through from Narmass once a month, passing by the ridge on the old Saugess trail. See it up on the bluffs? Foreigners like 'Osfore the Black' and 'Zerimes the III'—harsh rogues, prefer them young for their gizzards, which make potent medicines."

"This is enlightening news," observed Risgan.

"And you fear not Grinneth?" demanded Jakus with wild amazement.

"Ha! I offer the old cow the odd creature now and then. Just to appease her. Sometimes a treat in guise of a villain or two. Do you know of any wretches worthy of the honour?"

"Unless you like dead ones," muttered Jakus wryly. "We left poor Minc down on the shore a few leagues back. Couldn't see the use of transporting his corpse all this way."

The animal keeper gave a wistful nod. "I understand the sentiment, yet I will make a point of retrieving Minc's carcass at a time later in the week."

Risgan winced at the thought. He paused to examine the odd, unsettling surroundings. A choke of green ivy grew up the tall cliffs. The yard, once a common court ground, was now a litter of caged animals.

Straw, dung and jumbled stone pens lay everywhere. A series of water troughs radiated out from a battered hand pump of an old stone well which served to water the beasts. Square slabs, once brute-beast stalls, were crudely fashioned into other pens, stocked with goats, boar and wild chickens all behind mesh. The farthest dwellings—or store rooms—lay plunged in black shadow at the base of the cliff. A small fire pit smouldered off to the side, burning refuse or some foul rubbish, over which a large black pot of grizzled fat sizzled, leaving a faint reek of smoke in the air.

"I am the sole entrepreneur of this yard—*Borhoff*, my animal compound," the keeper announced proudly. "Who are you?"

"I'm Risgan. This is Jakus. We were besieged by fog earlier today and the ignorant wiles of Kraul the Crab, and here you have us, the only survivors of the *Yaster's Revenge*. I, too, had my bout with Grinneth on Vishfike's Isle where the sea witch met her final demise, much to her dismay. A betterment for the universe, if you ask me—facts which my comrade mulishly opts to refute."

The animal keeper glanced sharply at Jakus. His expression hinted that he had heard many tales of similar nature, very tall ones at that, spoken by rogues and simpletons. With a weighty sigh, he spoke, "Well, my grandfather, Vevis—he was a notorious pirate, marooned here on this beach long years ago after a peculiarly fearsome struggle, likely not dissimilar to your own. Perhaps a strife over a marauding caravel? Bah, my memory is dim. Vevis had no taste for worldly life and founded this zoo, which later my father took over and I continued the tradition. I could charge admission for my efforts, but the lack of folk frequenting these areas makes the idea rather impractical. As you see, my menagerie is eclectic and available for viewing without cost." He extended a brawny arm in a manner of affected pride.

"A boon, certainly," remarked Risgan. "You are a lucky man, Lubdar. I envy you! You have an environ all for yourself. How does it make you feel?"

"I feel splendid. Long before my grandfather's time this stone village used to be part of lord Raznor's domain: *Weremist*, 'twas called. Regard the cracked tower on high." He pointed two fingers. 'Tis a rare sight, its octagonal thrust, its singular archwork. In those days Raznor's kingdom consisted of a thousand men-at-arms. All was at peace. The strength of the lord kept the lands free from sea raiders and conquerors by means of archers posted on high in his keeps in the cliffs. The village was sacked five hundred years ago by the Sea Kayads and is now what you see today. Raznor's towers have all but fallen—or lie dismantled or mouldering like snakes in the grass, as most of the kingdoms in these parts."

"A sorrowful situation."

"'Tis." The animal gatherer scrutinized Risgan with curious wonder. "You look antsy, Outlander. Has a bee flown in your behind or something?

Risgan heaved a brisk sigh. "If you want my opinion," he intoned, "I think your practices of animal husbandry are reprehensible. Only recently I chastised a certain villain who kept a menagerie such as yours, though somewhat less ordered. His treatment of lizards and isks was abominable. In fact, I see an ironic parallel. For instance, the gibbeth encaged in its sordid condition, quivering in its own dung. I could probably cite other instances of abuse worthy of report to the animal authorities."

Lubdar gave a sarcastic chuckle. "Do you now?" He uttered a rude croak.

"I do," declared Risgan, "and I shudder to think what resides in that caveish structure yonder."

"Your imagination wanders, wayfarer. Come, and I will show you. 'Tis only a depository where I keep a few trifling minor animals. I indulge you, if only to prove a point, and relax your tensions.

"Only for a minute then as other concerns beckon."

Lubdar bowed. "I am at your service."

While they walked over to the compound, the animal keeper demanded, "Isks, you say, Outlander? I have plenty of isks in the theatre back of the cliff. Do you care to see them?"

"Perhaps another time."

"I am sorry to hear such hidebound views of my menagerie. Here at *Borhoff* I demand high standards."

"That is a matter of opinion. Jakus and I think it is time for us to be on our way."

"And miss my prize exhibition?" the animal keeper leaned forward in indignation. He crinkled his face into a wincing grin. He seemed not to wish his guests to depart so early. "There is more that I wish to show you—if you care to linger. I will show you in my central cages my marsupials—"

Risgan waved a curt hand. "Nay, the sun arches low. Beasts will be wont to wander at such hours—"

"'Tis nonsense! The beasts are tranquil until midnight. One more room," he whined. "We are half way to the repository now. I receive none too many visitors in these parts, and truthfully, my pride would be bruised."

"Well, if you put it that way," grumbled Risgan. "Jakus, let us peer upon one more room then we must take pains to continue our journey posthaste to Namass. Nighttime falls and as I have intimated, I do not wish to be caught flat-footed in the dark by horrors such as those caged in your yard."

Lubdar gave a wild laugh. "They are as harmless as hens! Come."

He warned them against cages with the carnivorous parakeets that hung from rock pillars. "Mind your heads. The fowls' beaks are sharp and like to jab out and snatch flesh."

Risgan acknowledged the warning with a crooked mouth.

They approached the slab-sided cube, a structure fifteen feet wide by twenty long. The storm room appeared embedded in the cliff itself, likely some type of wine cellar, he mused.

The zookeeper pried open the heavy wooden door with a stick leaning aside and with a smile and grunt, jerked it ajar with a creak and an unsettling air. A wash of dank vapours poured forth and Risgan held his nose while Lubdar, neck jutting out like a crane, strode bravely in. The relic hunter reluctantly followed. Jakus brought up the rear warily. Eyes quickly adjusted to the gloom and Risgan blinked incredulously. He was aware of scuttles, surreptitious movements, the clicking of legs and the scrape of carapaces. Pale, luminous eyes shone from the dark which confounded his senses. Several bizarre creatures dwelled in those moving shadows here in this closet—to be specific, malamanders, land crabs, onyx-turtles, vokryes and more. All shunned the light.

A yard away Risgan saw six starfish pasted to the wall, glistening with a rare effulgence. He poked his nose closer and bridled at their sulphurous discharge. "I do not wish association with these things," he grumbled. "I've lost my love for the sea." The only light came from the doorway, a heavy portal which was slowly creaking shut on its own.

"These specimens are only mictomorphs," announced Lubdar disarmingly. "They are a curious breed of anemone and starfish which crave the dank of stone over the coldness of water. Each creature is worth a mint on the open market. In fact, I have an old sailor's story to tell of them, which shall wait for another time."

Risgan grunted his approval.

The animal monger gave Risgan a slimy grin. On a sudden signal of hand, a lepro-snake with large triangular head dropped from the darkness to engulf Risgan's shoulders. Coils pinioned his arms tight.

Risgan gave a great yelp. A grinning head levelled to his face, while tongue flickered; it eyed Risgan with a sinister intent. The relic hunter was rendered speechless with terror.

"Oh, ho!" cried Lubdar. "Events proceed down different channels. I see you have fallen afoul of Elgbret, my pet python. What a fair fortune! She roams freely in these precincts. I've had her from a young snakeling since my youth." The zookeeper laughed affectionately. "I warn you, Risgan—please do not make sudden movements. Elgbret is sensitive to jars. They tend to make her nervous. Ah, the trickiness of the rascal! All this excitement has made her somewhat flighty."

"Please unfurl me from this serpent this instant," cried Risgan haughtily. "I resent this treatment." He thrashed and squirmed, heedless of Lubdar's advice to remain still. Elgbret held him fast, using a stone projection as an anchor for her tail.

Lubdar laughed again. This time he tugged at his chin in thoughtful appraisal. "The configuration is somewhat fanciful, I daresay, Risgan. It adds value to the room. I think certain sharp words which were traded earlier still rankle on my memory. What is your opinion on the matter, Jakus?"

The shaggy pirate, eyes narrowed, spoke in cautious tones, "Admittedly, Risgan's grimace and the snake's complacency does add a certain charm to this dim burrow."

Lubdar slapped his thighs with a mirthful yelp and clapped Jakus on the back. "Jakus, you are a clever man. I wish I could spend more time with you. Unlike this young baboon here, you do not yap off at the mouth like a cornered ferret. Risgan has plenty to think about. Let us repair to my ventrilium."

Jakus demurred.

"Don't be shy. 'Tis off in the old crypt quarter. We shall have us a merry lunch, perhaps a few tidbits, while Risgan cools his heels here with Elgbret. I have other treats to show you: egrets, spinfets, marsupials, a rare set of jongers, fishrikes and basilhoons galore. Pets only, I assure you. Rarities as these are not fit for public viewing."

Jakus nodded with nervous comprehension. "My eyes are saturated, Lubdar. Perhaps another time. Truth be told, I grow weary and have seen enough animals for today."

"The devil you have! I was just about to introduce you to Visbiz, my finest aardvark. And this is what I like about you, Jakus: you exhibit a taciturn frankness, not like this lank-toothed cretin of yours. Often I am a most eager host and tend to miss out on the little signals that guests provide for my edification."

Jakus gave a polite acknowledgement.

"Hoy, and what of me?" bleated Risgan heatedly. "Am I to decorate this glum mausoleum, become plaything for your reckless amphibian who flicks an acidulous tongue at me?"

"Hush, Risgan! You are far too talkative for a man in your position. 'Tis always about you, you, you. My plans are yet unresolved; I feel a poignant inspiration coming on. Yea, my hogs are hungry! They crave human meat. 'Tis not common knowledge that the breed commands high prices. Here, I can afford some quality victual for them, from time to time."

Jakus breezily acknowledged Lubdar's reasoning. "Diet is an important factor when it comes to considering raising healthy animals." He took the keeper's argument in stride, remarking that the bumpkin Risgan had so far been a tiresome companion, owing to an intellect of low order.

Lubdar sadly acknowledged the truth. He fumbled with a coil of rope hanging on a peg on the wall and tied Risgan's wrists together. He clapped his hands and spoke a soothing word to Elgbret who quickly unfurled her coils to return to her midnight perch. The zoomaster circled Risgan's ankles with a bit of loose rope to inhibit any excessive mobility.

After prodding Risgan out into the yard with his hunting knife, he beckoned Jakus who straggled behind with some uncertainty. The pirate's brows were damp with sweat and his mind worked feverishly. His face showed a sudden insight and he uttered a cheery grunt. "Before consigning our guest to the hog pen, we should at least strip him of his valuables before throwing him to your hogs."

"A sensible plan, Jakus," agreed the zoo keeper. He gave his chin a thoughtful rub. "I'm pleased you mentioned it."

Struggling in his bonds, Risgan put forth a wheezing protest. "This is a low dealing, if I've ever seen one. You'd be better scoundrels than men. Lubdar, you are better off letting me walk free and lashing this other rogue tight with whithe. Jakus will cut your throat the first chance he gets. At least I harbour some integrity."

The animal keeper considered Risgan's request with a good lip-chewing. He turned a piebald eye upon the grinning Jakus. "I sense a certain truth to this assertion, but nay, I have made up my mind. An ancient Lingarian saying is best remembered: 'better the rogue we know than the one we don't'."

Risgan gave a facetious laugh. "And the corollary, a rogue who keeps pet snakes is an ill one indeed, especially one who encourages hogs to chew on one's legs."

"Oh, you are too dour, wayfarer. Much too dour. Lighten up."

While grunting merriment, the two rifled Risgan's pockets and discovered several lucrative items: several sets of dice and the knife which Jakus coveted and Risgan's weapons' belt which Lubdar snatched up in a flash. "The leather is fine here and shall suit me quite well."

Probing further, the animal keeper gave a warm cry, "Hoy now, what here? A pretty gem! What a fine idea you had plundering this rascal, Jakus. I think now I shall guard this keepsake. The bauble shall fetch a high price when old Fargar rolls through *Borhoff* in a fortnight or so. The old codger is a curio-monger and he commands a double wagon."

"By no means!" cried Jakus. "The jewel is my property, as 'twas my idea to frisk the ingrate, if you recall."

"A wild claim, Jakus. This demands some examination."

"No such examination is needed!" the pirate affirmed fervently.

The animal gatherer pulled back the gem with a weary sigh. "I see that I must speak explicitly. Your mewling does you no credit, Jakus. In fact, I retract some of my good comments about you. Your demand violates the first axiom of all good traders—that 'first to find is first to keep'."

"Rubbish, you filthy zookeeper! I see that blood must spill before reason hits home. Prepare to die!"

"'Twill be your blood that spills first, you peacock," roared the collector. He pushed down on the pommel of his sword, which was strapped smartly to his belt.

Jakus became overconfident and overstepped, perhaps pumped up by his recent escape from Kraul. He sought to end Lubdar's life with a quick stab with Risgan's knife, but the oaf stumbled and the animal trainer kneed him in the groin. Jakus fell and the zookeeper dove on him with practiced ease. Quick as rain, the zookeeper produced a rope and wound Jakus's wrists very tightly, much to his hoarse protestations.

Seizing Jakus's knife, Lubdar gave a hearty laugh. The blade came slicing down to shave off Jakus' left ear. "That's a good lad, that's for getting uppity. Oh, you must excuse me! My eye is not so good, ever since old Drake, my spider monkey, took out my left eye." The zookeeper gave a roguish guffaw, shaking his head in a wild rhythm at the memory. While Jakus howled at the loss of his ear, rubbing his earless cheek in the dirt to assuage the blood, the zookeeper whistled a merry tune, and in a moment of almost whimsical chivalry, he wrapped a rancid rag around Jakus's ears to staunch the bleeding. "There now, don't say that I didn't do anything for you. Up into our cage, my little birdie!"

Jakus quivered with pain. Risgan was ordered to squat where he was.

Lubdar, casting thoughtful eyes about, saw Jakus's pink ear lying in the sand and retrieved it, wrapping it in a soft cloth. He whispered slyly to Risgan, "One never knows when scraps like this will come in handy. In fact, old Deerdeer is likely hungry. I think I will add it to his meal as a special treat." He tossed the ear far and it landed within the caged confines of a nearby captive hoo. The grey, snarling creature shovelled it up in his maw, much to Jakus's howling dismay and Lubdar's laughter.

"A good day's work done," crowed Lubdar happily. He marched over to his hog pens, which were many and stout and reeked with a hundred stenches. The animals grunted in fitful waves, smelling the blood. "There now! It seems as if I have two rogues to sacrifice to Grinneth," he remarked idly.

"Grinneth is dead," Risgan muttered. "Did you not hear?"

"A pity." The zookeeper rubbed his chin. "Well—this bodes well for you. You have done me two services, Outlander. I need not satisfy the avaricious demands of Grinneth, and I get to sell you for a princely sum to the next slave trader who comes trundling through *Borhoff*. A caravan is slated for next week." He scratched at his cheek in musing and looked up in the sky. "Well—up and into the cages, you stubborn badgers! Besty and Hugus died last week of dropsy and I can spare the extra cagery. I don't see why you can't occupy their stalls for the time being while I mull over this quandary of what to do next. Briskly now! I am not a man to idle when I have captured new hauls."

Pushing Risgan forth at sword point, the zookeeper listened as Risgan conveyed his criticism of the deplorable treatment. He more humbly suggested that Jakus occupy the closest stall, which stank of the vilest odours and contained the most effluvia.

Lubdar tilted his head in reflection. "I had not thought it mattered, but I will heed your request."

The pirate Jakus and Risgan were thrust in their respective squalid cages, so low that they had to squat. The wooden bars were clamped tight. The locks snapped shut.

The two glared glumly through the pales while Lubdar stooped briefly to examine the stone he had acquired from the relic hunter's purse. Shaking his head in surprise, he peered at it in more queer fashion than ever. The relic hunter took opportunity to apprise Lubdar of its special powers. "I wouldn't touch the bauble, Lubdar. 'Tis a talisman purported to grant youth and vigour—but there is barely a whiff of magic left in it which I wish to utilize for my own purpose."

"Think again, rascal." The older man gave a pitying laugh. "I shall spare you the effort and take a generous dose myself. I am hale in nature, but my bones creak from time to time and certain mild youth serums might do me some good." The animal keeper gave a jovial grunt. He heaved his bulk erect.

Risgan made a slow show of protesting the zookeeper's extravagant expectations. "I have not only lost my pride, but my life!"

"Oh come, Relic Hunter, enough of your melodrama!"

The animal keeper was fascinated with the bauble and as he turned it over in his hands he seemed like a child mesmerized with a new toy. At times he squinted at it with his one eye; at other times he tested it with his teeth, all half dozen of them while murmuring wildly and somewhat nonsensically. Risgan grinned on with thoughtful speculation from the safety of his cage. His frustration finally began to abate.

It was then that a strange thing happened. The animal keeper suddenly paled and twitched.

Risgan leaned forward with interest. Lubdar began to jerk and writhe. Perhaps it was the sea brine which had contaminated the nephrite?—reacting with it in some alchemical way?—or the excessive handling that the animal trainer had given the gem. Whatever the case, Lubdar's hair became thicker, shinier, like a glossy pelt of an earlier age. He was a young boy; then the opposite: he was an old man, his hair thin and grey, his bones shrinking, his skin wrinkling. The zookeeper lurched like a drunken madman, clutching at the gem. He staggered sideways, seeming unable to control his motor functions. His hair grew alternately ever ranker and greyer. Then he tottered, fighting to right himself again. He fell again, legs splayed, rasping out a hoarse cry aside Risgan's cage.

Risgan regarded the bewitched man with only passive interest. The contrast of age differential? The effect of the cursed magic on a despicable psychopath? Either way, it was inexplicable. By extraordinary means, Risgan managed to thrust out an arm and paw at the twitching body. He located the key in the man's pocket and managed to jimmy it into the cage's infernal lock. With scrambling haste he kicked open the door and crawled out, groaning with exultation. He stood peering about, his lips parted. He inspected Lubdar's yard with an attitude of loathing. The motley arrangement of creatures and outbuildings caused him to bare his teeth and think many things. The creatures sensed a new change in the yard and they mewled and snuffled in hope. Jakus watched from a distance, a strangled hope dawning in his breast. He gave Risgan some sugared encouragements and mouthed advice on his path to freedom.

Risgan ignored the demands. After a while, the retriever grew tired of Jakus's sycophantic calls and thrust in a stave to silence his whining. He plucked up the youth talisman and pocketed it. Careful to give the zookeeper wide berth, he blinked in critical distaste. On second thought, he gave Lubdar a resounding boot in the groin, which prompted a high-pitched yelp. The animal-monger stared vacuously at him like one of Zanthia's detestable ghoulmen whom Risgan remembered so well. Risgan retrieved his gleaming bodkin and weapon belt from the sordid keeper's person.

Now, matters had assumed a more equal bearing and Risgan gave a lordly laugh.

He was alerted by telltale squawks from the teratyx cages and remembered his proven skill at riding one under the tutelage of Ferios at Bazuur. He hustled to examine the ring of four cages. Several large beasts with thirty foot wing spans skulked within. He selected the healthiest, most promising beast.

Jakus's hoarse croaking voice drifted out of the shadows of a nearby lone cage. "Come release me, Risgan. Where are you? Loose me from this abominable hutch. The key is not far on the zookeeper's belt. Would you leave an old friend to die?"

Risgan mustered a satiric frown. "I would, and if I hear any more yammering, I might consult Elgbret."

Jakus opened mouth to protest but thought better of it.

Risgan freed the bird. Clambering on its back, Risgan massaged a special area behind the teratyx's ears. The bird cooed and responded with an arch of back. He squeezed with both legs and the beast took off at a shambling run down the beach. Within the space of a breath of air Risgan was airborne and gave a wild yell of exultation. His lean flanks swung up over the ridge. He was flush now with the watchtower and he saw its ancient face grinning back at him, scored and cracked, and cleft with its dozen archers' slits.

The yard below grew smaller as a honeycomb maze of stone and wood and Risgan spied Lubdar having another odd fit. The zookeeper climbed to his knees and shook a gnarled fist up at him, a much older and grimmer Lubdar.

Risgan gave a merry laugh. Jakus, confined to his small hog cage, was glummer than ever, and Risgan gave him a respectable salute. Doubtless the treacherous backbiter would come to terms with his new life.

2: Ravenna

Risgan flew on the back of his teratyx swiftly. The weather was fair; the wind had died. The honey-coloured sky ran with white clouds that floated like big birds. Risgan soared over the rugged lands, carefree and content, away from the troubled sea. Below, the seaside cliffs slipped away in green ledges and the blackstone keeps with it, so much were they the only memory left of Raznor's heritage. Yet Risgan saw more castles inland: abandoned black octagons with single towers from whose high battlements arrows would have flown in days of old to defend against sea raiders. Farmers' fields of yellow sea oats passed below, fringed by dense woods and with goats grazing in the glades. Far to the north a ridge of high mountains glinted of glacial peaks.

Risgan passed over what he thought was the hovel of Alvzar, the slum village that Jakus had mentioned. Nothing more than a mere hint of an ant hill from this height but he kept on to Izbar, the richer settlement that was likely a gateway to Namass. Market squares spread below with dignified stone residences, a passable road which wound in from the west over a sparkling river. It passed through a scatter of hogback trees and disappeared into a blur. It would be advantageous to fly the bird on and seek out ruins and places of plunder, but truthfully he held no ozoks, and he was famished.

The reconnaissance yielded worthwhile data. Risgan eased his beast down into the cobbled marketplace where several merchants gathered to greet him. Astonished faces blinked in the sunlight, surprised to see one so proficient with the teratyx—most arrivals flew in on balloons, or trundled to the market by caravan. This being the case, Risgan had no trouble selling the gleaming beast for a sizeable haul to four animal traders from Namass.

He rubbed his chin with gratification and inspected his handful of coins, suspecting that there was more to be made in the teratyx-trading business. Yet the thought of returning to *Borhoff* in a more rigorous search deadened such ambition. He recalled the diabolical Lubdar, and the evil waft of degeneracy that lay heavily over the zoo of his creation.

Peering left and right, Risgan discovered Izbar to be a small trader's settlement at the banks of the river Zind. Feeling somewhat invigorated by his recent dealings with Lubdar and Jakus, Risgan thought to start up his old practice of relic-gathering. This exotic region specifically had the look of promise from the air. Risgan's first priority was to rebuild his arsenal of relic-hunting supplies: first, new pickaxe, scraper, burlap sacks, appropriate clothes and hat which he purchased without second thought. He had been through this exercise in the past, and with such frequency that he could perform the actions in his dreams.

Market news was rife. Only a few casual inquiries yielded that an old temple of Vitus with modern-day disciples was stationed no more than a few leagues north and west in the forest district of Hagus and was ripe for spoils.

Risgan nodded with satisfaction. Before he could act on the impulse, an enthusiastic gentleman hustled up to him—one with bright eyes, a beaming face, scrubbed and red, and neatly attired dress of blue and white suit, a look which proclaimed the mark of a possible businessman or sharper.

"Excuse me, sir," the man said suavely, "I could not help but notice your dramatic entry into the Hagus market. The bird you sold, 'twas for a high price. I trust you are satisfied?"

"What of it?"

"A man of funds. Now that we have established that, a moment more of your time. You look a high mortality risk man. Under my discretion, I wish to tender you a valuable offer."

Risgan peered critically at the parchment the man clutched in a fist. "What's this?"

"A type of 'death by misadventure' insurance—'tis an extraordinary benefit which protects the heirs of wayfarers from untoward inconvenience. 'Twould guarantee funds to pay for a coffin, a proper burial and headstone and wreaths. In your line of work, surely you have lain awake at night fretting over how your corpse will be dealt with upon your demise?"

Risgan gave a half-choking bark of laughter. "'This business is not for me. The concept is morbid."

"Aye, too many feel this way, not just you! But for your family members who must necessarily scrimp and save..."

"I have no family. I suspect that when I die, I will die in a lonely place; there will be none to mourn my passing, and no one to gather my bones."

"The possibility exists, yet—"

Risgan held up a firm hand. "No buts. I am busy. Certain business attends, and I must depart."

"Very well." The man's dejected expression sought to arouse pity and he turned away with bowed head.

Risgan shook his head in sad wonder. Touts of this kind were stretching the limits of decency, preying on a man's vulnerability and fears to peddle insurance.

The man, however, was not to be so easily put off. He returned moments later with a flushed face and a conclusive finger raised high in the air. "If you will, sir, sign on this line and extend us a measly eighty ozoks into the fund, all will then be in order! That's a fellow. I think you shall thank me in the end."

Risgan gave a high-pitched growl. "Are you deaf? Must I resort to my cudgel?"

"Disaster is an imminent part of life and my guaranteed certificate is an important commodity!"

Risgan grinned with surly humour. "Perhaps, but as I've indicated, 'tis not for me. What if I'm gutted by a gibbeth or wrapped in a kodo's tongue somewhere out in Lim-Lalyn? Who will then collect my mangled parts—or the insurance?"

The salesman opened his mouth to protest, but then closed it with a scowl. "There is little likelihood of this. As I hinted, these are rare happenings which normally occur one in ten thousand and constitute fringe theoretical cases—"

Risgan raised a threatening hand. "Be off with you! I will never submit to such idiocy... now make yourself scarce, rascal! I am becoming impatient and as I have already intimated, I am famished and have important things to do."

Crestfallen, the salesman shambled off, shoulders slumped.

The audacity of such swindlers caused Risgan to grit his teeth and he wondered what next would come his way.

Only two more incidents assailed him, relatively minor. Tired, he lay over at an inn, the *Barrel Box*. The next day he commissioned a local farmer to take him by wagon to the Vitus temple. The cart driver was happy to oblige; he himself was en route to Bazlan, to sell yams and eggs... Risgan sat slumped between chickens and bags of potatoes in the back of the farmer's wain. Cramped aside the gear, Risgan contemplated life's ups and downs, and how fate had brought such a humbling downturn in his career.

Somewhere along the road, the farmer stopped the wagon. He lifted a finger to a patch of old daedilias and motioned to Risgan. "There, wayfarer—past the copse, you will see ruins of Old Vitus. I venture on to Hagus and then Bazlan. Good luck to you! I hope you find what you are looking for."

"I too, and I echo the blessing. May you find green pastures." Risgan scratched the top of his ear and snatched a look at the vine-ridden wood that crept out a bowshot away amongst the thick grasses. He tipped his hat to the farmer and wandered a path through green flower weed and fallen logs, then he found an old foot trail that wound deeper into the forest. The trail was marked with ancient stone, flags lay palely visible in the weeds, so overgrown and buckled it was.

Risgan broke out of the trees and arrived in a glade of grassy mounds and toppled columns and statues.

His eyes swam, drunk by the sight. He stumbled spellbound upon the old columns of Vitus—the temple, he reasoned—purportedly dedicated to an eccentric saint of the middle period of *Weremist* history. He studied the ancient columns with interest, that lay strewn in the grasses. Old underground stairways were covered with moss and sediment; rank twitch grass had completely taken over bygone pathways of stone, in a graveyard of time out of mind.

He recalled the locals at Izbar telling him that the ruins of Vitus crouched at the feet of an older settlement of Hagus. He trained eyes up the wooded incline. Near the summit, he saw a forsaken castle of ancient blackstone standing above the forest. It was a haunting sight, a structure of three turrets with collapsed basilica, a patina of moss and crumbled tile, the last testament of the old rulers of Hagus, a lineage long since passed out of memory.

Risgan climbed a quarter way up the hill and saw a purple band of mountains to the north, the same that glistened with snow peaks that he had spied earlier. In the distance, the crags belied the starkness of the moss-covered ruins to which he now put his attention. Returning to the valley, he grunted with exhilaration, selecting a promising recess amongst the toppled columns and desolate acreage, a half-buried stairway, upon which he let fall his pickaxe. The rich red soil would lead down to unknown surprises.

In the bright of day, Risgan found it easy to summon courage to dig for such relics on this possibly blessed soil. Not ten paces away, a drunken statue reared, on whose plinth rode cursive script too old to name. Only faint memories lingered here, and forgotten spirits, thought Risgan. Solitarily he dug at an opening which yielded under his muscled strokes. At the first sound of metal striking stone, he grunted and wiped sweat from his brow.

A young woman chanced to approach, perhaps an acolyte of the temple, alerted by the sound of his treasure-digging. She clutched a basket of elderberries and spoke with a faint whisper. "What's this, thief?" she cried hoarsely. "Why do you quarry on our temple ground? Get away before I call the monitors!"

Risgan grumbled out a fiery note: "Away, Sister. You wouldn't want to start meddling in things over your pretty head."

"I'm no meddler!" she cried, stamping a foot. "I shall report you to the Konar himself."

"Gads, I'm trembling in my boots," Risgan breathed. He leaned heavily on his pickaxe in an attitude of amused sport.

She clenched her slender white fingers into balls. "Are you ignorant of the fact this is the hallowed ground of Canthras? The modern temple lies half a mile away. We worship the glory of Vitus there."

"A worthy ambition. Can't say as if it tickles my fancy. One saint is much like another."

She gasped in shock at the sacrilege. "You blaspheme Vitus?" Her face pinched in a frown; she was ready to run when another woman appeared from behind a ring of crumbling columns. "Alaxa, please go back to the adytum and your prayers; I shall handle this stranger."

The newcomer flashed Risgan a shrewd inspection, and not without a certain lively interest.

Risgan sized up the woman himself with his own cunning gleam of eye. She was beautiful, looking like no acolyte he'd ever seen, even while dressed in the loose robes of a senior nun with her golden buttons and lace, contrasting sharply with her lustrous raven hair and its fine-woven braids. A fire burned in her features; not a servile one, or in any way religious; only a fierce intelligence was projected in those eyes and her outward presentation was infectiously vivacious.

"You know—" she suggested blandly, "you might be better transferring your digging to that mound yonder. A lucky treasure-hunter like yourself might come across a pretty stash—at least, that was what the last plunderer said, before he was caught by the Konar."

Risgan frowned at the second mention of the Konar and debated whether the information was true or not. He peered cautiously at the site in mention. "It seems a potential prospect. Small worry this Konar—"

"Quickly now!" she hissed. "The head monitor, Culax, will be sauntering by on his walk before noon. He scans the ruins for defilers looking like you. He is fractious. You have no recourse but to leave. One hour you have. No more!" With a flourish, the woman was gone in a flurry of white robes.

Risgan, deciding that to take up the alluring woman's suggestion would not be unprofitable, decamped his current project and with a carefree shrug, set to industry on the projected mound, a curious tract behind a toppled architrave. To his delight, his pick struck pay dirt, clinking on a trunk of notable items: a brass tube of ancient scrolls, a multicoloured medallion, two ancient copper tureens, three bronze censers holding ceremonial candles... And so, Risgan's labours did not go unrewarded.

The temple groundsman did come bustling from the north as the woman had predicted, like a busy beetle, through the straggle of moss-eaten columns. He was a smug, troubled man with shaved head, waxed and gleaming, thickset build, red-striped robe and philosopher's beard. Risgan convinced himself that he was some caricature of an acolyte's dream. He was just finishing up covering the hole he had dug when the official came trotting by.

Risgan hid his sack of valuables and tools behind a fallen slab and sat down on a mound of earth nearby. He put on a semblance of innocence, thrusting a piece of grass between his teeth and granting the monitor a friendly salute.

The man halted to fix Risgan a cold stare. He could spy no evidence of thievery. The monitor passed on, feet thudding like a young didor's.

Risgan grinned, pleased with his work. He inspected his curios with an air of finality. He tied the neck of his sack tightly so that none would spill and for a time he wandered the ruins, stumbling on another overgrown footpath that led him closer to the modern-day temple.

He found the lovely young maid as before polishing silver cupware with a delicate hand near what looked to be the outer part of a small worship chapel. Perhaps it was a shrine. Risgan gave her an appreciative stare, which she did not seem to mind.

Risgan tossed several thoughts over in his mind. Not the least of which included amorous roughhousing with her. Curious that such acolytes or slaves would drudge here on these desolate ruins, Risgan stared about his surroundings. He assumed the larger temple lay on the other side of the stout brick wall that ran perhaps a few furlongs away.

He hailed her and asked her of her duties. She turned her back on him coyly and continued her work. She seemed to polish her cups with an energetic zeal. Risgan thought the act peculiar and could not repress an amused grunt. He snapped an instruction at her. "At least turn around and look at me."

With great deliberation she placed the cup on the altar and regarded him with solemn inquiry.

Risgan thought to attempt a pleasantry. "I thank you for your suggestion, kind lady. It seems I have chanced upon a nest of lucrative spoils. Here, take a look!" He held up his bulging sack.

The woman hissed at him to put it away.

"You don't look too proficient at polishing," he observed with a frown.

"You are a perceptive man," she muttered dryly. "The devotees of Vitus drink from these cups." She pointed to a particularly old one. "When the spirit of the Saint reveals himself, 'tis said that blessings come through the wine. I reside at the temple for other purposes..." She fixed him an enigmatic stare which grew to a somewhat heavy vulpine interest in his broad figure, and not an unflattering interest.

Risgan did not miss the nuance.

"I have," she added, "been known to dally with a strapping man from time to time, much to the shock of the Konar, if he were to ever find out."

"This Konar sounds like a dull sort," Risgan grumbled.

"Aye, he is." The maid's insinuation was surprisingly frank and left Risgan with a hanging jaw. He arched his brows and put on his most suave manner. "And what would such dalliance bring, Miss Goblet-polisher, you who are a sight loveliest to the eyes? Short-changing your duty at the monastery?"

The maid's lips curled at the remark. She hummed a sly suggestion. "I can think of other activities that we might engage in, wayfarer, superior to polishing cups—" a suggestive motion brought Risgan's eyes toward the nearby sanctum.

He regarded the wood-peaked shrine with new interest. The sweet, charming sway of the maid's hips was by no means overdone and he approached her and ran his hand through her raven hair, admiring the tinged highlights of deep violet there. Her exquisite features showed silver-green eyes, long-lashes, aristocratic cheeks and a sensuous mouth which inspired Risgan to the maximum indiscretion and he began to trace circles on her slightly wetted lips with his fingers. The woman was of magnificent figure and height, standing as tall nearly as him and he could see her exposed limbs plainly in the sunshine, arms and thighs strong and supple, arms sunbrowned and slightly oiled and gleaming with a radiance that belied her chaste outer-bearing, showing under the loose robe.

Risgan pried his eyes off her body. The covered chamber served as a convenient trysting point for the two. Within seconds both milled inside. The interior contained a thin pallet for kneeling on and a pad for conducting prayers of devotion. There would be other devotions practiced today. A thicker, reed-woven mat she pulled from under the altar and lay aside in the centre of the room and Risgan, not wishing to be a dullard of some kind, doffed his vestments and clutched her with amorous anticipation. For an hour they made excellent play with their time. During the swift interlude they enjoyed numerous luxurious embraces and intimacies beyond the call of the norm—all in the relative privacy of a holy room. Then, Kraul's wrath!—only to have their congress interrupted when the naked maid gave a steamy call, claiming—or rather warning—that Culax, the monitor, would be returning in no time.

"Who cares about that dull sod?" Risgan cried, clutching her bare shoulders. Yet seeing the worried look of the girl, he donned his garb and stepped out into the sunshine to reconnoitre the area. With a lazy yawn, he stood gazing in blank rapture. Ravenna covered her luxurious body and pretended an easy manner, returning to her cup-shining enterprise, while Risgan plunked himself in the shade of a stunted mangrove, well off the main path.

The monitor, half unexpectedly came clambering by from a different direction this time to give Risgan a familiar searing look. He seemed suspicious of the way in which Risgan whistled and how he gazed up to admire the breadth of the sprawling mangrove trees and the collective of young female acolytes not too far away. They stood poised across the wall, engaging in odd chores on the temple grounds. All the while, Ravenna looked down with ever flushed face and continued to polish her cups with a studied intensity.

The monitor strode off with grumbling reservation. He barked orders back at Ravenna to hurry up her polishing, which seemed to be taking an inordinate time. In a distant gazebo Risgan could barely make out a large man in blazing white robe and red conical cap rattling a ceremonial sceptre and regaling his audience with familiar maxims and prompting murmurs and coos from witnessing votaries.

The relic hunter restrained an oath.

Ravenna's brows rose in surprise, perhaps amusement. "I see you are no mooncalf, treasure-hunter. If there were more time, we might engage in more playful frolic—" Her eyes flashed hungrily over his youthful, well-muscled body and her thoughts danced dangerously to and from the sanctum.

Risgan held up a hand. "Another day, lass. I might visit the town first and amuse myself there before returning. This fine temple of yours poses intriguing possibilities. I have certain business to attend to in Hagus, the like of which can't wait. Is there anything of worth there seeing?"

The maiden brushed back her damp tresses. "There are the baths, of course, where maids delight in administering massages and healing touches to men. There is also the oracle of Mileak; more a glorified fortune-teller anything who gives a detailed synopsis of a person's life, at outrageous cost, of course." Her face was flushed, full of flirtatious radiance and Risgan liked what he saw.

The baths would constitute a footling diversion, but in the end, Risgan gave his head a dramatic shake. "Truthfully, the local alehouse is more my style. Nothing like the dim lamps, the telltale clink of mugs, and a warm beer in a man's hand. Not to mention languid women."

"Have it as you will," she grunted shortly. "I will be here all evening, if you care to dally. Come early, but I can guarantee nothing after ten. If all goes well this evening, I shall never polish a wretched cup again..."

Risgan thought the remark odd but he shrugged his shoulders.

An awkward moment followed and finally Risgan gave a clumsy salute and strode on his way.

Yet he could not bring himself to leave. There was something eerie about this place and he knew he had seen this temple woman before. Where? The minx had the beguiling raven eyes and the shiny black witch hair of a figure he had once known... But for the life of him he could not remember...

"Dress like a monk," she hissed after him as he struck a path toward the modern temple.

* * *

Risgan came to the end of the ruins where ran the low brick wall. Under a carved archway he passed rows of flanking statues and was granted entrance into the main temple precinct—what looked the heart of the modern worship-grounds of Vitus. Low alabaster fountains tinkled with cool waters on neatly trimmed lawns. A covey of small birds flitted in and around, tweeting and drinking. Elegant gardens were rich in flowers and vines while manicured shrubbery edged the pathways radiating out to key sections of the temple grounds. Three or four columned complexes rose within the park interior, shaded of ancient daobobs, also a massive old stone cube which looked more like a crumbling mausoleum than a fane, almost as old, or older than the ruins in which Risgan had been recently foraging.

Risgan frowned. The structure seemed out of place here in this sculpted oasis of perfection. In the nearest grounds, plaques were erected on podiums at regular intervals and inscribed with legends describing St.

Vitus's deeds. Here was one that drew Risgan's attention. He read aloud to himself:

"We commemorate the miracles of the great Saint Vitus—martyr, healer and kind-hearted being. The station of Wellbeing marks the 'Miracle of Wealth', a feat which occurred a league away at Hagus. Coins suddenly appeared from the saint's cuffs, as if by magic. Vitus gave them all to the needy orphans of Demphes and the lepers. This wonder happened on the 12th day of the month of the Didor, 866 CD."

Risgan scratched his chin. Most admirable! he thought. He studied the statue of the saint with deeper reflection: an iconic monument of ancient grandeur that accompanied the plaque. Small sparrows sat on its shoulders. Young children were depicted playing at his feet. Men and women of all walks of life had come to bless the saint, prostrating before his sandals, which seemed reputed to harbour some mystical energy and were looked upon with holy regard.

Risgan's eyes narrowed in a scowl. He respected a generous man no less than any other. Yet he remained sceptical of all the hoopla regarding miracles and touted by followers. Many magicians could manifest coins galore in greater profusion than poor Vitus here from far more singular places than sleeves.

But he was not here to judge.

Passing within listening distance of the opulent rotunda where the fat man spoke, Risgan could hear the sum total of the devotees' chanting. Male and female were conjoined in solemn worship in the rotunda. Unison voices rose in an eerie hum. He could not suppress a certain humour for zealots, but remained curious as to their motives. It seemed that Ravenna, so-called acolyte of Vitus, was up to some mischief here of her own, perhaps other than worship... at least so he suspected from his limited exposure.

Devotees were milling about the pavilion now: bald men in white and gold robes and white-garbed women with lilies and red gems in their hair. All were arranging flowers, candles, prayer beads, cups of sacred wine on the altar. The pavilion was surrounded by white columns amongst which the members busily weaved their way, whispering and trading fleeting nods. The columns were carved of alabaster in the sober taste of old Venamesque. Red draperies coated the back wall. A red-and-gold-blanket covered the altar which took centre stage. A door of carved wood loomed off to the side, doubtlessly an avenue to the inner adytum.

All persons stood to attention. The mighty Konar began giving a sonorous lecture, an overbearing man with rich red robe and rings on his fingers, and decked in his red conical hat. At times, the speaker would stroll purposefully about the pavilion to adjust candles, criticize the attitudes of acolytes who had lit the sacred flame too abruptly. He chastised them for their careless positioning of religious items, or their dress.

A most uncompromising man, thought Risgan. Watching the proceedings from afar, Risgan thought to detect an air of unease in this a singular group. All members seemed to wear the same solemn expression of servile lassitude that he recognized elsewhere, as if worried about committing an offence against the Konar, or Vitus himself.

Risgan grunted a small chuckle; he retraced his steps to hop the wall not far from the main gate. The reason was neither impractical or theoretical: the entrance was watched by two burly monitors. He took to the dusty road to Hagus, for the afternoon was wearing.

* * *

The blackstone towers at Hagus were renowned for their thick antique stone, well-preserved, unlike most of Ranzor's decrepit ruins. The town was smaller than Izbar with only a few crossroads, narrowed backstreets and mason-shops, a smith-forge, a few bakeries and not much of a market. An old stone well rose sullenly in the central court where travellers from Namass came to water their where-backs or refill their canteens. The footworn cobblestone court was a meeting ground flanked by blackstone bastions. Risgan deferred trying to sell his holy relics here: it was not the right place, nor enough of a merchant town to command and decent price. In all likelihood, his wares would create a controversy should any of the acolytes or temple monitors get wind of the source of his wares. Risgan still guarded ozoks from the sale of his teratyx and he thought to lie low, indulge in some important business, perhaps even visit the baths, if the pub turned out to be substandard.

He chose a small inn with trim wood siding and an iron sign that read 'Pauper's Pub'. The name befit his style and seemed well attended by wayfarers, a stop too which most of the locals seemed to frequent.

The taproom was bright and airy and Risgan ignored the noisy bar at the back, seating himself at a table with what appeared five locals. They huddled by the front window and seemed to be enjoying a lively game—a derivative of Sea Blackey if he wasn't mistaken. A prominent gentleman gave a respectful nod to Risgan. He was sable-haired, slant-eyed and wore a curved sword at his belt. The other was tall and taciturn, a lore-man of some sort, or some mystic or stoic. He seemed absorbed in deep thought. Another, was a certain heavyset man, who wore a moniker's cape and white-hair pulled back that fell loosely over freshly-oiled leather jerkin. He was garrulously invested in the game and showed the beginnings of liver spots on his cheeks and forearms. The other players were roustabouts: squat, bearded peasants, wearing worn garb in accord with their long faces.

Introductions were made. Risgan sat back to assess his new company.

"I am Skarl," the white-haired man announced, "—smith of Hagus. This tall, saturnine scholar is Pasilpun, a seer and sage of the highest order. There, Erling, the mayor's squire, and here, Balsrog and Daseo, important people in their own right."

Risgan acknowledged the introductions. "I am Risgan, an eclectic collector of intriguing things, no less a stalwart wayfarer."

"A rare privilege! But do you harbour silver, sir Risgan? We do not engage in frivolous games."

Risgan pursed lips as if anything could be further from the truth. He hefted his bulging sack of new relics. "Regard this and be amazed!" He jingled the sack with emphasis and made it seem as if it were filled with coins. "These are my wagers! See them and question no more."

Skarl nodded respectfully. All players seemed impressed, with the exception of Pasilpun.

"We usually deal with smaller bets in the game's onset," Erling remarked.

Risgan gave a puzzled frown. "You'll have to make some exceptions then, won't you?—or are you all a bunch of pantywaists?"

Skarl pushed his nose forward. "Here, now, wayfarer, let's have none of this language! You will see our mettle is as fine as any!"

"Good then. Let us begin. My fingers ache for play." Risgan's remark seemed to create a stir. Several were savvy enough to observe his gambling addiction in full force.

With no ado Daseo dealt three cubes and four disks. "Risgan, you do not drink?"

"Tonight, I abstain—perhaps even fast. It keeps my wits about me... a pretty female awaits my return."

Erling and Balsrog both nodded in understanding.

Daseo gave a coarse mutter: "Utter nonsense! Arrack thins the blood; it also loosens the wrist!"

"Do not forget, frees the mind!" bellowed Skarl.

Risgan gave an offhand wave. "Perhaps for you, but in this case I must remain adamant. You do not know this maid. Deal the tokens and bid."

"As you wish." The gambling led to theological talk, including discussions of death, judgement and morality.

"If I throw one stone up, it must naturally come down," announced Erling in a voice of proud conviction. "So goes a man's life, after he is born, so he must die."

"A profound observation, Erling, which presupposes the existence of a static, fixed universe."

"Ah, Daseo, you are much too shrewd a man of the world." Erling gave a hearty cry and slapped his peer soundly on the arm. "You could have been the Konar himself."

"The Konar... You insult me by associating me with him," Daseo growled peevishly. "I would not step a hundred feet before that crew of catamites."

"The game gathers spider webs, sirs," Pasilpun clucked. "Now less insults and more chips in the pot."

Risgan half-murmured to Skarl: "Your sage seems a severe sort."

"You are new to our ensemble, Risgan, a visitor from out of town. Therewith, Pasilpun will always remain a mystery to you. Pray thee, your token pile is full and fresh, which avails bids and action."

"You have a keen eye, Skarl, which will fare you well in this game. Guard your wits! You are pitted against an adept, who has seen many hard games in his day."

Skarl flourished his fist full of chips to indicate that the comment was redundant.

Risgan took pains to educate Erling: "At first I gamble these small ceremonial objects—" he pulled one of the incense censers he had unearthed out with emphasis "—heirlooms and bibelots only! They appear as old trinkets, but for a fact, are worth a mint in hard cold ozoks. I hazard to guess you must grant them full value."

Skarl frowned. "Possibly so, but you must find a dupe gullible enough to purchase these oddities at a high price. I, for one, value these soil-coated gimcracks at no more than twelve ozoks."

"Agreed!" cried Risgan with decision. It was six more than he believed he could get for them. "Let the game begin!"

"Patience!" cried Erling. "You drool like a schoolboy seeing his first love in the schoolyard. At Hagus, we do things differently, in unique manner, gambling fastidiously and with calm decorum."

"A worthy philosophy, but a proper game should fly by like the wind!"

Skarl shoved a fistful of multi-coloured disks under Risgan's nose. "Enough of these maxims. Well, will it be Varlets or Vassals?"

"Varlets, of course," asserted Risgan with dignity.

"Erling, deal our new member his four chips—the blue, red, green and yellow."

"Vassals, are now 'live'," Erling announced with pride.

Pasilpun, the tall saturnine gambler with long yellow face affected a percipient leer of indifference. He sat back unruffled and watched the play as Risgan's formerly decent luck began to turn sour. He lost round after round. More of his recently-unearthed trinkets passed into the hands of his grinning peers.

"How is it that you weasels always win?" asked Risgan in wonder.

"There is no mystery," explained Skarl. "We play in the company of Pasilpun, the magician—see how he remains so steadfast? His fingers are swift, and his delivery is like deft weaves of spider thread."

Risgan took no joy in the elucidation. "So we have a magician in our midst? First a sage, now a conjurer? Why did you not tell me of this earlier?"

"And spoil a game of good faith? Players are players. Prejudices foul a game."

"This concept is flawed!" argued Risgan. "I will argue that 'Pasilpun' is an illegal entrant. Yet he is not alone," Risgan hissed slyly. "I am a magician myself. Look! See this medallion with the seven colours? 'Tis one of a set— the seven crystals of the Savant Yarsax, favoured of the god Minatu who was recently endowed with tremendous powers of luck and fortune." He rubbed the Vitus relic with hissing vindication until it seemed to shine with a glossy effervescence. "Now! Let us observe. I will use this emblem to turn the tides of a lopsided game to colours in my favour!"

The others drew back with apprehension.

The company's throws were shakier than normal and predictably Erling and Daseo lost the trumps in back to back succession—with the exception of Pasilpun, whose hands stood fast, and who suspected bluster on Risgan's part. The magician remained composed, and the moment he saw Risgan's worthless 'medallion', he gave a sober grunt.

"Why do you not lose with us?" whined Skarl at Pasilpun.

"I am a magician," intoned Pasilpun. "I use counter-talismans to guard against Risgan's bravado." He produced a shinier, more opulent version of Risgan's medallion.

Risgan uttered a gasp of disapproval. He repudiated the introduction of thaumaturgical props in a game of skill.

Pasilpun seemed unmoved by the opinion and laughed at Risgan's own posturing. The magician seemed to make a negligent gesture with his fingers. The chips he dealt and the trump disks seemed to slide from his long slippery fingers like birds.

Risgan made an appalled exclamation. "What was that? I saw a most peculiar and unnatural hand dealt. Thaumaturgy reigns!"

Skarl refuted Risgan's qualm. "Merely a bizarre coincidence. Ignore Pasilpun's legerdemain and play on."

Erling chimed in with confidence: "Yes, Risgan, your outbursts are distracting us. Your own hands seem to have degenerated these last few rounds, despite your eloquent boasts."

"That is because I am busy watching Pasilpun's magic fingers!" retorted Risgan. "Who knows what other chicanery he is up to?"

"Ignore it!" finalized Skarl.

The other four players began to rack up wins and Risgan's few ozoks dwindled, which he was forced to put forth in lieu of relics—and which lessened even more much to the players' excited glee and grins.

Pasilpun returned an impassive gaze to Risgan's stare. He nodded from time to time at the others, neither showing the underside of his chips or spilling ale on the table like his bibulous peers. Risgan, who at this point was scowling blackly, was losing wager after wager.

Finally he flung down his chips in rancour. "I refuse to play on in this arena of cheaters which is rigged."

"A bold claim," stated Skarl. "'Tis your call, especially after losing most of your ozoks and relics. The 'Varlets' have deserted you, eh, Relic Hunter?"

"Do not speak to me of 'Varlets'. There are plenty of these in these quarters."

"Ho! You would resort to slander?"

"My mind is somewhat preoccupied," muttered Risgan. "The charms of an arresting maid infect my concentration."

"This is understandable," Skarl said without sympathy. "Now... we wish you the best of luck with your maid and we will be thinking of you in utmost diligence." There were murmured guffaws and grins. It seemed no secret that a penniless vagabond was about as attractive as a June bug gone belly-up.

Risgan gave a sour grin. He set his hat on a jaunty angle and departed the tavern with only a quarter of his relics. None of his ozoks remained. Not for the first time did the relic hunter regret his impetuosity.

* * *

By now, dusk was nearly upon the lands and Risgan, remembering the sensual embraces with Ravenna, made good speed down the dirt road toward the temple. A sceptical scowl curled his face: the maiden's shapely form seemed too unusually engraved on his mind, no less her luxurious heat. Risgan paused to assess his wrap of dirty woollen robe and greyish cowl. They were the only accoutrements he could find akin to any monk's garb in Hagus. Would they be adequate?

Risgan slowed his pace. The followers of Vitus's temple were engaged in a rite somewhere within the grounds. He stood a hundred yards from the entrance where two stern-looking monitors manned the gate. Always monitors! Each was dressed in the formal gold and red garb of miniature Konars. Risgan did not wish to raise their suspicion, and so he scaled the wall at a junction not too far from his previous point of exit.

He congratulated himself on the tactic, if only to maintain a vestige of mystery, for now he proceeded unaccosted on a diagonal slant across the foot grounds, following the sounds of soft music. A mellifluousness wafted in the air—the tinkling of bells, the piping of pan flute, the whispers of devotees, the spit of candles and wicks burning in old wax.

Early evening stole over the lands and Risgan saw the western sky plumbed with dusky amber and the forests plunged into shadow. Insects began to chirp and bats to swoop. The last fugitive light fled from cracks between the clouds and Risgan's sneaking led him to a pavilion back of the woods.

He followed the sounds of chanting and came to the *Temple of the Rose*, as it were—a three storied prayer house whose stair wound up to an upper loggia where stained glass windows and golden pilasters streamed with glimmering candlelight.

The lower floor was open, supported on columns. The great Konar was delivering another of his moving sermons on a raised dais, showered with light from jewelled lamps sputtering in hog's oil—the nature of the talk, on the sins of carnality. Risgan, from this distance, could feel the weight of the orator's mesmeric presence as he wooed them with his prophetic principles. He waved a multi-jewelled sceptre, the shank rich with garnets, rubies and amethysts, mounted with a large white pulsing stone—it was a globe alone worth a fortune! But Risgan could not help but believe that the magic exuded from the ornament itself, and not the speaker's spiritual presence.

The Konar intoned rich resonating words whose echoes reached Risgan's ears: "Good people of Vitus! Troubled times are upon us. The lands teem with gibbeths, the cities fall into a tumble of ruin and decay. See for yourself!—boroughs falling, mouldering, vines encroaching and gobbling up our civilizations. Even so, the site of old Vitus lies forgotten and neglected. It is sacrilege!"

Nods of acknowledgement were forthcoming and the members of the audience stood enthralled with their hands clasped to mouths and brows.

"And why, you ask?" intoned the Konar with air of finality. "There is a spiritual reason for this—'tis a malaise which afflicts us adversely. It enters our hearts, taints our souls and pollutes our minds. To this, we, as Vitus's followers, must apply our intellect!"

A wave of murmurs swept through the gathering. Risgan skulked closer amongst the manicured shrubs. His face was carved in a scowl. The Konar craftily waved his sceptre in free form. All eyes traced the bewildering arcs like a cat would a toy.

"So now, listen! Why are we so often led astray by vices of gross nature? We cannot control them, let alone fathom such temptations. I, as thirtieth Konar and Lord of the conservatory of Vitus, avow to have conquered these impulses! I come before you as a sterling pundit, an unsullied savant, a benevolent leader of gifted temperament, invested with the blessings of Saint Vitus. The great Sage has spoken to me! Many times He will speak again in his clarion voice of virtue! Let us throw down our mutual ignorance, surrender ourselves to the glory of Vitus, and lift high our arms to the heavens!"

There was a mighty chorus of cheers and acclamations to the declaration: rapturous, indulgent applause. Hands lofted in the air. Amongst the four-score devotees milling in the temple, not one naysayer protested. The men were mostly bald and the women, draped in their simple whites and reds, wore hair coiled in topknots, oiled and varnished like waxed seashells. Risgan could not repress a grunt. Such piety was lavishly pointless. He could hardly believe such a mindless throng existed. That Ravenna would run with such a crowd troubled him. But he could be wrong about her. To his relief, he could not see her amongst the flock.

He snuck around the back of the pavilion, not wishing to alert acolytes of his presence, entertaining a small hope that he would find her there, or perhaps discover some plunder to replenish his dwindled supply.

One of the white-robed acolytes tending to a mini altar in the after-alcove was not acting to cue. He saw, not surprisingly, it was Ravenna, silhouetted under the dim candlelight. Her curves were unmistakable and her stylish grace. What was she up to?

He crept closer. The maid was laying votive offerings on the candlelit altar, but somehow, something was amiss. Risgan frowned. Sauntering out from his place behind the bushes, he approached cautiously in a band of grey shadows where dew was just forming on the lawn. He wrapped his cowl tighter around his neck. He hesitated.

Why was she so absorbed in her duties? Better yet, why was he so captivated by this beauty? She was just some long-legged young pupil taken in by a cult. Her earlier remarks troubled him: *I reside at the temple for other purposes.* He had been naive, he realized. Not to his surprise, he caught a glimpse of her stashing certain ceremonial candelabra and gold chalices into a small silken wrap hidden from sight. Ravenna kept looking around nervously.

So! A thief, he thought... Not was he the only 'curio-snatcher' in this world. Surprised that such pilfering would be carried out by a her, one of such ravishing allure, he thought to startle her into a fright and snuck up behind her and touched her on the shoulder. She jumped slightly, uttering a muted gasp. Quick as an adder, she brandished a poniard, nearly carving off his nose.

Risgan jerked back in surprise. Despite the near slash, he could feel the blood pumping in his veins. A vague wolfishness curled across his lip. The temple maid was stunning, even hypnotizing, despite her violent reaction. By Kraul, where had he seen her before?

"Fool! I see you are easily inclined to sneak up on an unsuspecting mark," she hissed.

"No easier for you to rationalize your thievery," Risgan remarked heatedly.

Ravenna muttered her scorn. "This is the Brimsbane altar, a place of worship blessed by the Konar himself."

"Ah, good. I was just about to ask. Noted for its fine gold too, I bet," muttered Risgan.

"Who are these zealots but a batch of ridiculous sycophants for all their wealth and gold," she said with an unpleasant smirk. "With nothing better to do than throw their coins at religious statues, hoping for a quick passage to the gods."

Risgan grinned. "You sound embittered."

"You think? Aren't you appalled by the spiritual materialism here?"

"Not overly. I have other complaints—namely a certain depraved psychopath at *Borhoff* who comes to mind. He is—but I digress..."

Ravenna grunted. She seemed to intuit that Risgan was not going to do anything rash and she whispered to him in a conspiratorial tone: "I'll allow you brief opportunity to share in the spoils, but under no circumstances must you attract the Konar's attention. It could be the ruin of us both."

Risgan nodded. He raised two fingers in trust. "I am contemptuous of such demise. To emphasize my conviction, I will solemnize the occasion—" and he wrapped an arm suggestively around her waist and pulled her tight.

She pushed him away with impatience. "This is no time for play! Pay heed! Danger lurks."

Almost as if by fate, an unexpected figure shuffled out of the gloom. Perhaps the monitor had sensed a discord between the man and the female devotee who busied herself at the Brimsbane altar.

Another grim official trailed at the monitor's heels.

"You—fellow!" He motioned at Risgan peremptorily. "You are acting unbefitting of a monk. Is everything all right?"

Risgan put on his best smile. "Things couldn't be better. A slight cough and hiccup truth be told, but otherwise all good." In the makeshift disguise of a temple novice, Risgan bowed, feeling moderately safe in his garb in the dim light. "I hunger only for the truth and chastity of Vitus, the infinite compassion of his holy sanctity."

The monitor acknowledged the celestial affirmation. "The pleasures of ecstatic Vitus are beyond this world. They will shower us with rewards, my son!—one must have patience and apply repentance."

Risgan bowed low with grateful enthusiasm. "It is with this attitude that I tender a naive hope."

"Your words strike a chord in our hearts."

"Wait, I've seen you before," cried the other thickset man, a short dumpy individual with weasel eyes and philosopher's beard. His eyes widened in recognition. Risgan realized it was the same monitor who had sourly observed him dallying with Ravenna.

"An utter coincidence," Risgan remarked gallantly. He turned his face deeper into the shadows.

His mate assured, "Come, Culax, do not be so foolhardy! We have things to attend to. Besides, there is not much time before the Konar's sermon is over, which means—" He snapped his fingers with a certain urgency and suggestive darting of eye. "These bushes shall do quite nicely." As if to prove the point, he had sidled off, but Culax had lingered to study the face which looked so categorically roguish and wished not to be studied. Culax reached out a hand angrily and pulled off Risgan's cowl. "Hoy! 'Tis you! You overweening imposter!"

Risgan felt his world clunk. He gave Culax a rough shove and a reeling fist to the skull which sent the monitor staggering to his knees. He toppled soundlessly like a stone.

"Fool!" hissed Ravenna. "Now we are both in a fix! Quickly! Drag this lug out of the light. Into the bushes before his chum Maribar returns."

With great effort they pulled the body off the dais and out into the bushes away from sight.

The official's colleague duly returned, searching for his mate. "Odd, I see Culax nowhere. Have you seen him? He has not caught up with me."

Risgan explained: "Culax went to gather some foxweed, I gather. You know how the Konar loves his bouquets set on altars adorned with fresh wildflowers. There were few in these gardens, I noticed them before dinner, but there are also many blossoms in yonder wood."

The monitor stared at him as if he were joking. "At this hour?" He pulled uncertainly at his chin. "Odd that Culax would attempt such a flamboyant display of devotion. Ah, well, he seemed somewhat flustered of late, something about a suspicious visitor he saw earlier today. Hmph—no matter. The night is—romantic." And he blinked suggestively at Risgan and let the hint incubate. Risgan curled lips in disdain.

Smoothly Ravenna interceded on Risgan's behalf. "Culax will be returning soon enough, Maribar. Best not to rile him with your flirtations. We should seek comfort in Vitus, or else temptation shall master us. You can find him yourself before he gets lost in the woods."

"A wise plan," Maribar agreed. He marched off in the other direction and was swallowed up in the darkness. Risgan resumed his earlier grumbling, mouthing curses at the monitor's barefaced forwardness.

"Hush! More are coming," Ravenna cried and pulled him aside. "Quick! Don this robe—" She reached purposefully into a nearby trunk to pull out a billowing red and white gown. "Look smart. Your piety and innocence and their persuasiveness determine our fate."

Urged by her pouts and hisses, Risgan swiftly did as he told.

Fearing the disguise too weak, Ravenna pulled him back out onto the central grounds. Risgan frowned at her haste. Yet the urgent look on her face hinted that she hoped to avoid the bulk of acolytes who might be loitering around the Rose Temple after the Konar's speech. Risgan took up her sack; in his other hand he clutched his own relics from the dig.

Out of a wide lawn they came around the Temple of the Rose to pass behind a garden path protected by odd-shaped shrubs. The sounds of the conference drifted in rising waves. Back in the pavilion, the Konar, his illustrious form backlit by candles, lifted his hand and lofted his sceptre. They saw it beguiling the eyes of all who watched. The hierophant's voice grew in a dramatic crescendo with the unleashing of the sceptre's brilliance.

"'Tis the globe that hypnotizes," muttered Ravenna. "See, the light renders his audience susceptible to his suggestions."

"Then, how did you escape its mesmerizing ability yourself?"

Ravenna hissed. "Only weak minds are gulled by such power. My mind is stronger than that. I pretend to be hypnotized from time to time, in order to achieve my goals."

Risgan nodded in thoughtful speculation.

"'Tis said the demimark Ekmartes fabricated the globe with the aid of his gemsmith, Ismiar, a genius of his time. The demimark wished to enrol women as those in the gathering that would bend to his wishes—women that he could never willingly have, owing to the demimark's particular ugliness and repulsiveness. The magic was too frail and Ekmartes ordered it modified by Barenes, a daul-mystic. Its power became even more sinister. Eventually, the globe made it into the hands of the Vitus cult, the Konars who, witnessing their power waning after the death of their patron, thought to gain more followers. The Konar of this day uses it for his own needs; shamelessly too, to convert dissenters. In fact, he personally relies on its function to attract helpless followers, so depraved has he become in his lust for amassing devotees."

"Oh, ho!" snorted Risgan. "Most sordid. I like this fellow less and less as you speak. Then, I will assist you in this venture of yours, if only to fulfill a certain quixotic cause."

Ravenna croaked out a hollow laugh. "You'll do nothing of the sort. Most likely you'll tag on to enjoy the spoils of the wealth."

Risgan shrugged. "You can put it that way." He scratched his chin. "You say the gems around the collar of this sceptre are magical and authentic?"

"Not only that, but priceless."

Risgan tugged at his jaw.

"Forget it," she mumbled, as if reading his mind, "the sceptre is guarded by spells, dark ones, I hear, beyond either of our means, and it is locked in its storage case."

Risgan had some experience in the area of spells and grunted out a protest. "If you're going to be a thief, you might as well be a bold one. The risks and penalties are the same."

"Perhaps." Her eyes gleamed in the moonlight. "Well, the sceptre is stored in the reliquarium, a hop and skip from here near the temple's mausoleum. After the Konar's sermon, his henchmen will take it there. We can be ready. His sermon is a long one, on the vice of temptation," she went on mordantly. "It will end in a quarter of an hour, or less."

"Giving us ample time to set up a trap," said Risgan. "We shall visit this reliquarium then."

She gave a small grimace, but seemed not utterly averse to Risgan's idea. "Swiftly then! We must get to the reliquarium first, if only to post ourselves inconspicuously in the dimness before the guards take their positions. It will be much easier to break out when they are not expecting us than if they are facing us in full force."

Risgan rubbed his chin in agreement.

The Konar's speech was curtailed, owing to other business at hand. The night gathering was milling about the columns now, chatting enthusiastically about the salient points, faces glowing in the high fervour created by the Konar's words. Some devotees filtered onto the temple grounds to repair for the evening; others conducted themselves to shrines scattered about the complex to perform supplementary rites.

Ravenna gave a muttered curse. "Mother Douran! Our timing is ill!" She pulled Risgan out of the way, down into the bushes. The tramp of footfall grew. She grabbed the sacks and tossed them into the brush and whispered at Risgan to act in a casual way. "Say nothing."

Three figures materialized up the flag-stoned garden-way. To Ravenna's alarm, the Konar was one of them.

The group approached with authority and made a grave inquiry: "Ravenna, you look flustered. Whatever is the matter?"

"Nothing, Divinity. I merely tremble in the presence of St. Vitus's energy—as you can surely see."

The Konar nodded at this with a sombre understanding. He removed his conical hat and scratched his bald pate humbly. "'Tis an understated emotion. This contagion of devotion leads us to moments of catharsis, which can only serve to enrich our lives for years to come."

Ravenna nodded brightly. She could barely suppress a retching croak— her low opinion of the Konar was wo low. But out came a strangled endorsement of how true the Konar's words were.

The Konar seemed to consider the praise with reservation and turned eyes upon Risgan, to give a troubled frown. "It is not like you to keep the company of monitors." He motioned to Risgan and squinted as if trying to recognize him.

The retriever, who had his face slightly averted, gave a small laugh and an inclination of head. "I allow it, Konar, if only to indulge the whims of an inexperienced novice. Ravenna here, derives benefit from my wisdom, which I give freely as manifestations of Vitus's compassion and blessing. I may even indulge in such counsel with other novitiates... though I have not yet decided on the course."

"This is the way of the true monitor. I admire your ethic, comrade," affirmed the Konar.

Risgan gave sober approval. In guise of a temple monitor, he bowed his head, speaking in a voice of humility while Ravenna gazed on sourly to the side. "I ache only to taste the nectar of truth and the boundless leniency of Vitus."

The Konar gave an all-inclusive sweep of hand. "This ecstatic ambition will be known to you soon enough, son. Persevere and continue your studies!"

Risgan nodded with rapt attention. He recalled that Culax had expressed similar sentiments, before he had been clubbed down.

The Konar passed Risgan, squinting up at him in the near darkness, fixing him a queer look. "You, Gavar, if I remember your name, seem uttering fine words this evening. I should bring you up on stage to deliver a small speech. But you look unhealthy and pallid. I suggest a half cup of spinach—raw, mind you. Cooked, spoils the man. Raw liquid does wonders for the soul and the complexion."

Risgan bowed. "Too true. You are only too wise, your Excellency."

"'Konar' will do for now."

"As you wish, your Excellency—I mean, Konar. One day I hope only to tread in your footsteps."

As if sensing flippancy, the Konar gave a curt nod and went on his way with his attendants.

"Well—that was a close one," Risgan breathed.

"Quiet your tongue, you cheeky glibster. You almost gave us away. Hurry! No time to lose." She grabbed his wrist. "I thought you were to stay silent. You are as glib as a eunuch; nay, a walking *perilnoot*."

To this, Risgan had no answer. They gathered up their spoils which they had jettisoned in the bushes and slunk alley-cat-wise down the walkway and through the garden. A veiled moon shone on the temple's columns, outlining porphyry and jade in an eerie combination. If the Konar were to know they transported sacred chalices...

Risgan thrust the thought out of his mind. Alongside the walkway they came to a smaller, unsettling mausoleum crowned with stone gargoyles. The damp stone gave off a musty scent. Risgan disliked it—it stank of decay, candle wax and incense of myrrh. A broken stair led down into obscure shadowy depths.

Risgan mustered a frown.

Ravenna spoke soberly. "'Tis the haunt of Slag."

"Slag?"

"Aye, it was said that Vitus, in his temptations, visited the underworld to befriend certain sub-world minions to assist him in defeating the evils of vice-spawned Ur Daklith. Certain devotees still believe to this day that the guardian Slag, one of Daklith's most prominent minions, is entombed below, but nobody has ever proven or disproven the rumour or seen the creature..."

"This would suggest extravagance on the part of the devotees," Risgan suggested.

"Quiet! Ur Daklith is the false lord. Certain sounds at night admit that the entity is real: whines, dread wails, hisses, grunts, gusts, other tumult which emanates from the crypt's lower precincts. Offerings are made regularly here to the creature, which are snatched as soon as they are placed, and never seen again.

"Then I can only assume there may be some validity to the legend," said Risgan, absorbing the information with care. "However, these myths are often crude embellishments of only trumped up wives' tales."

"Some, agreed," admitted Ravenna, "but they tend to often echo real events."

Risgan could not deny the possibility. He pulled himself grimly together, and away from the dank stone. He slipped a hand under Ravenna's arm and tugged her gently away from the shadow of the mausoleum, an act which stirred a passion in his heart. "Let us abandon these frightful surroundings and repair to a more private place, if only to engage in affection before we take our leave of this accursed temple. I hanker to resume our intimate connection, which I sorely miss."

"Are you deranged?" she cried. "I carry the sacred golden chalices wrapped in silk. I am a thief and could be hanged for unforgivable crimes. Do you forget where we are?"

"The Temple of Vitus. Do you think I am a half-wit?"

"Besotted more likely," she stormed. She gave an impatient flourish. "Then, you can carry them, along with the relics you pilfered from the ancient grounds. My absence will soon be noted and the monitors will come looking for me, wondering where all the ceremonial objects have gone to. We are hardly out of the frying pan."

Risgan could sense the real reason behind Ravenna's impassioned words and attributed her jitteriness to a mis-management of emotion, likely in the form of a suppressed longing for him.

He made a placating sound, nodding his conviction. "The gate and stone wall are not far off then. Let us quit this dreary place and retrieve the Konar's sceptre. With our new wealth, we will start a fresh life together and be all the happier. Easy to hop the stone and be out of this hutch before any of the Konar's friends is the wiser..."

Ravenna grunted offhandedly, but she offered no comment.

The reliquarium loomed high and dark, a bowshot away from the guttering flambeaux strung along the main gate. The thieves descended several marble steps to find themselves in an oval stone chamber dimly lit by censers. Several relics were on display—St. Vitus's skull, the saint's shawl, robe, scrolls, tomes and other memorabilia—all glistening under polished plates of glass.

Risgan pointed to the glazed bust of the man poised high on a podium in the centre of the chamber. "How did he die?"

"Some say Vitus was bitten by a scorpion or some poisonous snake out in the hinterlands. He was on a pilgrimage of hope. His last words were a curse to all serpents and stinging creatures."

"Doesn't sound very saintly. What do others believe... ?"

"That he was held at knifepoint by a band of footpads and killed for his valuables. His last words were—quote—and in light of his absence of wealth—'that there is no hope for humankind'."

Risgan reflected on the conclusion with no surprise.

Ravenna gave an exaggerated gesture. "Here are his toe bones, there his sash, a beggar's robe and whalebone necklace—Vitus's relics, his last and only possessions. The old mendicant's sandals with the scuffed leather and cheap lapis lazuli beads are still scored with the whip lash he received caught trespassing by the old lord Ventres in the town's square while giving a rousing speech to the peasants. Vitus, apparently, was known for these sandals... the old leather had travelled with him from town to town, spreading the Orlvord gospel."

"What's that?"

"A philosophy that insists the world is a cosmic egg, split by the dragon Ell. From the fissure spewed the moon, the sun and stars, the celestial bodies. Then the rain came and filled the cracks with water to create the oceans."

Risgan nodded thoughtfully. "An interesting theology. I wonder where the mountains come from?"

Ravenna gave an ironic grunt. "A poignant question. What of your own philosophy?"

Risgan laughed jovially. "My notions are so sketchy as to be embarrassing. Yet, I'm more apt to trust in the luck of a good club than a prayer bead in my right hand."

She wrinkled her nose. "A violent philosophy. Mine is richer: I believe that angelic mermaids crossed the great divide between *Fairth* and *Umo*, the metaphysical plane and the gross one between the real and the unreal dimensions. They created the world out of sheer whim. Inevitably the angels were carried away by the Abamorphs from a far planet because, being celestials; they were pure and worthy of much better than whatever could appear on earth. From then on, men came in hordes to ruin the planet."

Risgan blinked in awkward reflection. "The credo, though intricate, seems to point to the male equivalent of 'misogyny'. I suppose, every philosophy carries as much weight as any other."

"They do. Enough chatter! We have work to do—and a limited window of opportunity."

The two crouched in the shadows of the rear doorway—to a storage room in the back near several sacks in the shadows. Two monitors, solemn as pikemen, clomped down the stair and placed the sceptre upon its stand by the bust—a cushioned square of velvet on a stone podium.

Risgan watched with intensity as the two monitors secured the treasure in its brackets. Easy to unlock the mechanism. They covered it with a high glass dome. The relic was protected not by any spell, only a curious brass latch which seemed to work itself on the inside of the podium.

Risgan grinned craftily. The treasure was simple as dovecotes to acquire. No alarm need be made. When the two had departed, he secured the sceptre with ease and carefully replaced the glass, stifling a cunning laugh.

Ravenna, placated that no dark magic was in fact in play, composed a simple scheme to foil the guards who were positioned outside the door. They would surprise them by stealth.

Risgan saw the pair stood impassively outside the door to either side. Fearlessly Ravenna bolted out, prompting a cry from one of the sentries. Risgan rushed out on her heels. He cracked the laggard on the back of the head with the Konar's sceptre; the other he kneed in the groin as he turned to see who had attacked his colleague. Risgan and Ravenna quickly bound and gagged the struggling victims with ties from their sacks and pulled them into the darkness of the reliquarium. Wiping hands with satisfaction, Risgan took her aside. Luckily, no one had heard the cries. "We must take care not to run into any wandering busybodies with the sceptre in our hands. I cannot conceal it."

Crouching on a run, the conspirators were almost out of the compound when things started to go awry. The gate stood a stone's throw to the left— Ravenna with her gold chalices and Risgan with his sceptre and stash of relics and his heart beating with a thrill of the chase.

To their misfortune, Risgan, engrossed in sensuous daydreams of his new love, staggered too quickly around a bristle bush and crashed headlong into a team of monitors and attendants. They were carrying urns of grapes, sweetmeats and tureens of water; wine also at the Konar's bidding to his private chambers. It appeared that the Konar had planned an assembly with several other hierophants of orders from distant towns. The cult leader wanted to impress his guests.

One of the monitors yelled at Risgan, "You bumbling oaf!" He took hold of his senses and gritted his teeth. "You look unfamiliar." He stepped closer for a brisk look and Risgan paled, noticed that it was the mean, burly fellow he had seen guarding the gate.

Ravenna spoke up quickly, "It is only Dyang, your Lordship. He was accompanying me—to the outer temple, for prayer to Selban's virtues and the singing of Vitus's glory."

The other scowled his disbelief. "The temple is the other way, sister. Why are you so close to the gate anyway?"

Ravenna gave a forced giggle. "In fact, I am afraid I am at fault, fearful of shadows—the way is ill lit along the garden, but better by torches along the wall."

The monitor, Casius, acknowledged the truth of the assertion and gave a grudging nod, but his face clouded as if something was not right. "A strange coincidence then..." He peered at the two with growing suspicion. Risgan's robe and cowl had begun to itch abominably and in an effort to compensate, he felt it slip a notch as a watchful acolyte pushed a torch under his face. "Look, Casius, this is not Dyang!" The light revealed a man not bald but considerably more youthful and more rogue-featured than what a monitor should normally be.

"Who are you?" thundered Casius. Several others reigned in to inspect the mystery man.

"What business is it of yours?" Risgan growled.

"Ravenna?" another cried. "What are you doing with this imposter?"

Several attendants seized the struggling woman. She fought like a tigress, dispensing many bruises and bloody noses. But she was secured. Risgan, surprised at the maid's sudden vehemence and strength, decided he would not want to face her in a dark alley. The winded monitors gasped, glimpsed the gold bowls and candleholders and the emblems of Vitus tucked in her sack and they gave startled cries. They lifted them on high to show the lead monitor.

Ravenna stood, dishevelled and flushed, secured with strained impatience. Her half stammered excuses that she was taking them to the penitent's shrine for cleaning and polishing was scoffed at. "You are a liar and a thief. Both of you will go to the Konar and be judged. Perhaps whipped and imprisoned. Look! The sceptre of Vitus, half hidden under this man's dirt-stained robe along with another gem, a brilliant nephrite—'tis likely thieved from a rich noblewoman! Blasphemy! The Konar shall roll over in his bed when he hears of this crime! Xasis! Rnar! Fetch him now and tell the esteemed one that we have caught two filchpurses. You others—gather up these infidels and we shall bring them to the Konar's residence!"

Blows and shoves later, Risgan heaved a bitter snarl, "Here now, you cretinous dawcocks, this conduct is unbefitting of priestly men."

The outburst was ignored. Several kicked him in the ribs and the orderlies dragged him to the Konar's residence, a small stone cottage some distance from the main temple. Rosewood beams piled up to a conical ceiling.

Under the cold light of censers, the Konar nibbled at his grapes, appraising the guilty duo with an attitude of bovine curiosity. He spoke in a hushed voice, "How now, Casius, that you bring me such stray birds tonight?" Like his peers, the Konar was graced with a bald head, covered liberally in the red cone headgear of his order, which signified the gravity of his office. Risgan saw under the glaring lamps that his arms were plump, white and soft, but a powerful torso belied his foppishness even though he wore a small affected goatee that made him look like a pompous old billy goat. A company of four Hierophants sat at his side, surveying the thieves with attitudes of contempt.

"How is it now," he grunted jovially, "that the innocent lambs come to the slaughter?" He gave a rich laugh. "So the children of Vitus must learn their contrition? Luckily, I am a good shepherd, one who steer his sinners in better directions."

Ravenna seemed not to be comforted by these benevolent assurances as Risgan read in her features. He saw the beginnings of shock, even fear. The Konar's face was hard enough to make a dolomite statue look like wet clay. Despair crept over her visage and Risgan began to grow a trifle apprehensive himself. He struggled in the arms of his captors but was given short shrift and a solid buffet from Casius. "Cease your squirming, you filthy worm!" Despite their life in the temple, these bald flirting men seemed to be remarkably hardy.

The Konar, appreciating some of Risgan's inner musing, remarked in not unkind fashion, "I hire my orderlies specially from the outer regions. I assure you that they are trained competently well in the arts of subjugation, so please do not struggle unnecessarily, misguided one, else it will go ill for you. Alas, the world is full of opportunists—as Vitus has warned us time and again—they need to be tempered."

"Let him go!" sobbed Ravenna. "He's an innocent bystander. 'Twas my idea. I take full responsibility for the stolen items. Punish me as you will, but do not harm him."

The Konar tsked his tongue with a moved pity. "Very noble of you. You are far too maudlin a martyr, Ravenna, for such a sly rogue as this to go unpunished. Hush, child! Vitus would be pleased! I am overwhelmed at your sudden magnanimity and play-acting in saving your big bad boyfriend. Well, you blink at my claim? What a show! Release him? I think not."

The priest turned authoritative eyes to his orderlies. "The thief—throw him to Slag."

"Hold up!" cried Risgan. "Slag is a monstrous creature, I've heard. You rhyme off a grave decree."

"Slag sees all and is part of the divine pattern," agreed one of the dignitaries. "He will guide you to reason."

Another laughed with morose implication. "Aye, Slag will."

"The intruder will know truth," agreed the Konar thoughtfully. "And the woman—" he cast a lascivious leer in Ravenna's direction "—she can be put to more convenient uses. A saucy colt, she is, waiting to be broken. A nymph who hides under the guise of virgin whites of her nun's cloth. Ha!

What a charade. I know of her clandestine diversions in the shrines. A defiance lurks in this one's eyes which I will tame. I shall take the honour upon myself to educate Ravenna in the *mysteries* of Vitus."

"A good idea," acknowledged another hierophant. "I wish I were in your sandals."

The joke went not unrewarded but the ominous cadence of the Konar's words sent chills up Risgan's spine. He felt a jealous heat growing, owing to his recent lust for the girl.

"No!" she cried.

"Yes! Now silence, wench. Your fate is sealed and has been fore-ordained for a while now. You think I am oblivious to your absences from my lectures?"

The lead monitor Casius, indicated Risgan. "What of this goat?—" he gestured with an inclination of head "—Perhaps we could spare him for supplementary 'ceremonial' tasks?" The suggestion was indelicately posed.

The Konar frowned in displeasure. "No, Casius. I am well aware of your proclivities and 'extra-templar' amusements. For the nonce, I do not care to learn more; these thrusts and heaves in the dark night are generally insensitive and unbecoming of a Vitus orderly. Now back to your posts. My edict stands. Take the infidel to Slag!"

Casius bowed, lips quivering in crestfallen silence. "As you wish, Konar."

3: The Mausoleum

Blindfolded, Risgan was dragged out to the mausoleum; the five monitors hauled him down the mouldering stairs which led under the bowels of the crypt. Risgan could not tell where he was, only that the air seemed cooler, mustier, fouler, and that their group rounded many corners and traversed many dank passages, each more disquieting than the last. A fierce surge of pride welled in his gut when he recalled Ravenna offering to take blame for the crime. It was a courageous act. He admired her more than he cared to admit, standing up to the Konar and coming to his defence, something he would have done for her as well, had he thought it would have amounted to anything but a lost cause under the circumstances.

Risgan's captors did not take their leave of the labyrinth right away. They twirled him round like a top till he was dizzy to the point of retching, then they gave him several blows before removing his blindfold. He lay in aching stupor on his stomach, shaking his head of the daze, discovering that the monitors had departed. He lifted himself to his feet but found his jailors were impossible to follow. There wasn't enough light to see footprints in this eerie gloom, nor was he familiar with these tunnels; only a few pools of grey moonlight came shafting down from bleak notches high in the decaying stone. Risgan heard only trickles of water and the plaintive whines of a lonely creature from afar. He shivered. Such sounds echoed in and around the clammy confines with a despondent urgency.

Squatting painfully on his haunches, he looked about with distaste and alarm. The cry came in regular intervals—not far away, as if the owner sensed some presence of new flesh.

With small leisure, Risgan scrambled down the narrow, stone hallway. Three gloomy passages reared in his path, looming like gibbeth dens; each offered their own chilling possibility.

He pulled himself together. The middle branch seemed least nocuous and he negotiated his way down a twist of tunnel, trying to make the best of the sinister side corridors that gaped out at him. He was senselessly lost before he had taken a hundred steps. Sounds were muted in these passages: echoes of woe dulled by cold stone; his own footfall fell like the thud of hoofs. He stepped across a pool of filthy water, then across a strip of bare earth from which hung heavy iron rings mortared into the clammy wall. Perhaps they were for holding the ankles of an unpenitent man? Risgan tried to notch some of the columns that intersected the corners and T junctions with his small bronze buckle, but so far he had never come back once to the same column—which implied that the maze was more extensive than he imagined.

Risgan bit his lip; he still retained his acolyte's robe, but he felt chilled in this dank environment. There were too many passages to manage and he began to grow dizzy at the thought of wandering around here lost forever. He cursed the Konar. He cursed his insatiable relic-procuring curiosity and his manic lust for Ravenna which had landed him in this predicament. He pined for his wish bone, that which he had lost many weeks ago in the depths of Mangor forest—So many things he had lost in his life... loved ones, possession, and now the woman, Ravenna, for whom he felt an overwhelming fondness and to whom he felt a chivalric duty. He had failed to aid her and that saddened him most.

The sight of horizontal graves to either side of Risgan twisted him out of his glum reverie. Rows on rows of the sarcophagi were stacked, cut lengthwise into the stone walls. By dint of faint moonlight, he detected cryptic markings etched on the front of their slabs, signifying names, details and dates of saints, orderlies, and holy individuals of the venerated order of Vitus: Saint Cecum, Saint Hictum, Saint Marsberd of Averlis, martyred on 878 CD; Osibus, son of Nissem, pundit and soothsayer, laid to rest 891 CD... Inside the ledges Risgan discovered mouldering bones, tattered clothing, sacred objects, sceptres, eight-pointed stars, prayer beads, sphinx stones, medallions. Also untold symbols and writings that would puzzle the most learned scholar. Hearing the mournful cries echoing closer, Risgan escalated his scrutinizing. He restrained the urge to grab some relics up and flee.

Rounding a corner, he saw a primitive emblem carved upon an ancient lintel: two sinister serpents entwined in a spiral circle, each chewing the other's tail.

The sight caused him a grimace. Such sigils were known to instil terror and everlasting curse. Such a strange symbol for so benign a group of monks, he thought. His frown turned to a grunt of distaste. To his great alarm a heavy slab moved back. A false door opened and out of the dimness shambled a large sinewy hulk, some kind of a prehistoric monster with pale burning eyes.

Risgan choked, nearly falling back on his heels. He had no weapon, knew no passage in which to flee, nor how to deal with such a beast of prey.

The creature, however, did not maul Risgan immediately; the thing was some type of mini, three-legged dinosaur, Risgan saw. It seemed to emerge with unpretentious concern, commanding a long repulsive neck, purple and wattled skin, the neck encircled with an offensive collar of radiating spikes. Perhaps these were tentacles, Risgan speculated; in the end, he could not say. Two legs rode in front and one behind. Oval eyes large as swans' eggs began to roll back in its head. The creature had a large hound's snout, a scaly tail, black flexible tongue which slithered from its toothy maw and other features of notable unpleasantness. Risgan had seen equally menacing minions in myth, carved on the slabs of ruined temples: demons, demiurges, scourges—and yet, Slag's utter repulsiveness was not to be belittled.

The creature intoned: "Who are you?"

Risgan could barely recover from his shock. How could such a creature talk? Some type of unfathomable magic?

After a long pause, Risgan answered. "I am S-Salspear, the Rose Peddler. And you are Slag, I'm guessing?"

"None other."

Risgan swallowed his fear. He attempted with difficulty to regroup his thoughts. "Please do not venture a step closer, sir Slag! You have disturbed my rest and my breath is foul. Do you care for a bouquet?—No? Then I will depart this dugout posthaste and trouble you no more."

Risgan tried to retreat, but the creature would have nothing of it. He caught up with him, snuffling in his ear, hopping nimbly on its three flat feet, sending cold breath beating on the back of Risgan's neck. "Hold now! Where are you going, O timid wayfarer, and where are your flowers? You mentioned a bouquet. I see no day lilies or begonias."

Risgan gave an exclamation of surprise. "How foolish of me. I have forgotten my blossoms. No great matter! Honest Salspear will scoot back to his wagon and retrieve his choicest wares. Would you care for daffodils or lilies?"

"Neither!" the monster snarled, swaying its neck back and forth like a cobra. Its eyes seemed to loll about like a spinning top. "I prefer bartolibs, which perhaps do not grow in your earth-bound glades." A sinuous tentacle uncoiled from the undulating neck and casually embraced Risgan's shoulders, redirecting the fervour of his feet in a more favourable direction toward Slag. "I wish to conduct words with you. Normally, unannounced guests suffer terrible fates—at the hands of Slag. Arousing me from my dream is not an offence to be taken lightly. Last week I wrapped up a saucer-eyed, bedraggled thief in my tentacles one by one, so that he might cure a little. Then, I sat on his head and hatched him like an egg."

"The punishment is just," Risgan nodded sombrely. "A most amusing practice, I daresay, Slag. Still, I would feel better if I could retrieve my flowers."

The creature ignored Risgan's banter. "Most think my means merciless, until their heads are warm as jelly, or hard as cysts."

Risgan frowned at the image. "I assume then this is your domain?"

"None other." From the creature's droll chin drooped a stringy set of catfish whiskers. "I have been relegated to these quarters by subworld forces, ever since the fulfilment of Vitus's mission."

Risgan's eyes rounded in puzzlement. "What mission pray tell was that?"

"'Tis a long tale."

Risgan nodded knowingly. "It occurred a long time ago?"

"Three hundred years to be exact."

"I think you have been gypped, Slag, if you don't mind me saying. I'll leave this for you to ponder. But first, what are your plans?"

Slag hopped closer, eager to discover someone interested in his personal life. The creature seemed to half leap, to Risgan's amazement, not unlike a playful goat on its three stocky legs and flat feet. "My master, Daklith, banished and disowned me, after I generously granted Vitus entry into the subworld."

Risgan pinched face into a frown. "I have some knowledge of the legend."

"Oh ho, do you? Then the subworld interests you?"

"Not in any specific sense," admitted Risgan casually.

"That is probably for the best. The subworld is a cruel and harrowing place: 'tis cave-bound, with pitch black shadows, prickly stalagmites, burning bogs, spooks, disgusts, and all-round general rigour. Ur Daklith makes his throne on a pyre of black ghoul bones. Can you imagine? He sits on high on his brazier, heedless of the ice-cold that wafts from the icicles above or the red-hot flames from below. His subimps wail; they moan in the murks, waiting on him hand and foot while they grovel in his slops and filth. Fatuous fools! I was one of Daklith's lucky guardians, relegated to the far extent of the realm, manning the lych gate before Imiz-Don, the kirg-haunted swamps. There, I guarded the portal against entry, by smorgs, lizipusts, envoy bats and Serkenian poisoners. Ur Daklith has many enemies, you see. 'Twas the same place where Vitus the Victorious came as an angelic spirit and proposed a sally."

"This is an interesting tale. And you denied the zealot, of course?"

"By no means! Vitus is a pariah, a paragon of godly persuasion. The man is beyond knowing. Even to this day, I remember his gentle hypnotic eyes, soft amber pearls, looking into mine, and allowing me to see the light."

"Perhaps your master's banishment of you to the far realms was an implicit fear of your goodness, or basic denial of your faith?"

Slag considered the possibility, then stirred in unease. "The idea seems farfetched. I do not wish to dwell on the matter. In fact, I feel a teary sentimentality coming over me now."

"Naturally, and I sympathize with your emotion... and now on the topic of exit—"

"Are you sure you do not wish to visit the subrealms with me?" Slag inquired eagerly. "Straddle my back and we will make a foray."

"The idea is tempting but here I must demur. From the sounds of it, Slag, I can't say that Ur Daklith would derive much pleasure from my presence or your return."

"Perhaps true. The last time he had me chained and dunked in a fuming sulphur vat for three subworld years."

"That is a stark punishment for such a minor crime."

"Again, Ur Daklith is Ur Daklith. Now, are you sure you do not wish to visit the subrealms?"

"As I have intimated, I formally disavow any such privilege." Risgan peered calculatingly at Slag. "Now we have heard a lot of your past, Slag, but you still have not informed me of your current aspirations."

"Oh yes! I forgot. . . Well, truth be told, I have none."

Risgan roared chidingly, "What? You have no plans to experience the world?"

"None. The 'world' as you know it does not interest me. I dwell in shadows, watching time eat the 'world'."

Risgan opened his eyes in surprise. "This is a morbid outlook. And yet very inspirational. Surely you do not wish to miss out, for example, on the Obelisk of Duranth, or the Awakening of the Seven Stone Magicians at Mirdask—?"

"Nay! These are fools and simpletons in comparison to Vitus," the guardian stormed.

"Think, man! The city of Bazuur and its famous air balloon tours? You must reconsider! I have taken tours on the balloon ways—I tell you they are singular, renowned about the world."

"Perhaps passing amusements to frivolous folk. But invariably an intellectual vagary. I enjoy my labyrinth as it is—grey, murky and dripping with water. The setting calms me. On occasion the devotees feed me a soul or two to maintain my good favour, for which I am grateful."

"I think this is a disreputable pastime," murmured Risgan. "There are plenty of souls out there to feed on besides me. Why waste your time? I can think of a few others—namely the Konar, who supplies tastier meat."

The creature became interested. "The Konar! I have heard much of this wondrous fellow but never met him."

"A pity. He is plump and well-spoken. In one out of every five persons you will find a rogue, and he is one of them, definitely an excellent morsel for feasting on. As far as ambitions go, you could study the philosophies of the magicians—a particular Afrid comes to mind."

"Afrid?"

"A wizardess who boasts singular theories of intelligent automata."

The guardian responded tartly, "Admittedly, such a pursuit spawns a small spark in my ambition... as I've always dreamed of being a thaumaturgist—it becomes tiring serving as a lowly minion."

Risgan clapped his hands. "Slag, let me be your guide! We shall make a quick exit from this horrid den, meet the Konar and sip tea and attend discourses. Perhaps even Afrid will put in an appearance."

"Are these souls far?—I mean, these rogues and magicians—and this '*Afrid*', as you call her?"

"A jot and a jump."

"A caution: I grow queasy in open places with too much light particularly, or activity."

"An unwarranted fear, Slag! There is a local magician in Hagus, a certain Pasilpun, in fact, who'd be happy to make your acquaintance. A veritable idiot-savant in the arts of gambling too, a jovial fellow with a skill for the game and deep humour. His companions are Skarl and Erling. They are absolute larks and will regale you for hours."

"These people sound intriguing, and too the prospect of a bit of new scenery. I will try out your suggestion, Salspear, if only to placate my whims and then we will return to my labyrinth to continue our discussion where we left off."

"As is only expected," agreed Risgan. "You are an upright and intelligent citizen, Slag. You have my solemn word." And here, Risgan made the sacred sign of the Three Muses behind his back, which he had known as a child, useful in warding off pacts.

Following the thump of Slag's feet, the two marched purposefully out of the maze, around dozens of corners and dank crossways and dripping walls, up the mausoleum's stairwell, and around many twisting bends into the cool moonlight.

Therewith, Risgan politely led the guardian to the central temple grounds. The moon's glassy face had swung a high arc in the sky.

Many thudding steps later the pavilion came into light, illuminated by tall iron lamps hung from chains. Risgan ushered Slag grandiosely toward the columns. "Lo, the Konar!" he exclaimed.

The Konar stood a stone's throw away, anointing a toothsome acolyte's forehead in holy oil or some unguent by the altar. Slag blinked in confusion. Risgan grinned in feverish menace. The Konar's cheeks were visibly scratched and bare forearms and his face looked overly pale and withdrawn as if things had not gone well with Ravenna. In a hopeful moment, Risgan thought that his love and candelabra thief had escaped, or at least put up a decent fight. Accompanying his Holiness were four other assistant Konars, or High Monitors as they were called, dressed in golden robes and red caps. The officers attended the Vitus Konar in formal authority.

Risgan and Slag approached the gathering. Slag began to thump his tail like a gibbeth and his wavering shadow cast ominous fingers far past the pavilion. The acolytes attending the hierophants stared aghast at the approaching monster which reared up on its hind leg and showed its radiating fan in a display of challenge, such to cast a denser and larger shadow threatening to swallow them all.

"What?..." gasped the Konar. "S-Slag? How can this be? You escaped your mausoleum? Unorthodoxy unrivalled!" Goggling at the monstrosity, the Konar trembled in fear and barked out frantic orders to his acolytes.

Risgan remarked dryly, "Not as unorthodox as the dank warren you confined him to, Konar." He strode forth imperially. He urged Slag forward to the foremost columns. "The Konar awaits. Come, Slag. You have several important things to relay to our Konar and his coterie."

Slag began nervously, "Yes, well, very true." The monster turned to the group. "My friend, Salspear, has assured me that there are rogues here in need of devouring. And so, being a cooperative soul, I gladly oblige."

Risgan gave an encouraging 'here, here' at the declaration.

Slag, confused by the din stirred up by the acolytes, began to sidle uneasily back and forth.

A foolish monitor took it upon himself to threaten the monster with a jewelled stave and Slag struck out with a forked tentacle to lift the zealot to its mouth. Screams and shouts shook the gathering. The stalwart was swallowed in one fearsome gulp and others cried out in terror as Slag struck out at others, those nearest to the Konar.

The monster advanced with impartiality, disliking the brouhaha and the frenetic dashing about here and there. The other monitors and the Konar grew pale as ghosts and they turned on their heels and fled helter-skelter.

Risgan took the opportunity to scramble rabbit-like to the Konar's private apartment to search out Ravenna. But she was nowhere in sight.

The relic hunter's heart sank. Where had the beautiful maid gone? Her linen sack of treasures had vanished; his own sack of valuables and youth talisman were clumped upon the Konar's polished table. These he snatched up without a second thought.

He glanced about. He saw a lithe, supple shape slide by the window along the shadow of the wall. The shape disappeared—past the view from the window. The dense kagbushes grew in numbers, and Risgan thought the shape could be anything. He ran out, creeping like a fox around the bushes, following the trail of the elusive form. Had he imagined it? Risgan looked again, blinking uncertainly in the glow of flambeaus. Ravenna was nowhere to be seen.

Risgan's heart pounded, full of doubt. If it were her, likely she had made off with the Konar's treasures. He hoped it were true.

Sounds of pandemonium issued from all corners of the compound. Slag, in a fit of fury, attacked without restraint. The guardian had gone berserk; it was harrying monitors and acolytes without restraint. Was it the moonlight shining in his eyes that made him so mad? Perhaps it was their disrespect for the underworld minion which had aided Vitus so long ago? Risgan doubted either. Masonry cracked and roofs imploded to the thrusts of the monster's powerful limbs and its dragging tentacles. Cross-slabs toppled like bowling pins and the bawls of men reached his ears, not to mention the hoarse cries of women.

Risgan quivered with dread. What had he unleashed? He lay flat on his belly in the long grasses by the rough-bricked temple wall. Cursing his predicament, he wished only that he were anywhere else but here. Under no circumstance must he allow Slag to catch hold of him...

He heard the guardian's voice boom above the destruction. "Where is Salspear—my double-tongued *friend*, Salspear, the Rose Peddler?"

"We have never heard of him," cried a beleaguered monitor. "You must be deranged!"

More crashes and booms drifted to Risgan's ears, a clamour of animated shouts and screams of terror, which excited his imagination.

"Find me the Rose Peddler, or I will raze this temple to the ground!"

"The fellow does not exist!"

Risgan ducked, wincing at the sounds of Slag's tumult. To linger in this doomed quarter was an act of reckless stupidity. He gave up his search for Ravenna. The reliquarium was nearby. In a sudden burst of speed, he fled into its unmanned confines. The sceptre of Vitus glinted dully on its stand, in the dim light. He snatched it up and whatever other relics he could find, stuffing them in his pockets and jamming them in his sack.

He scrambled out warily, searching for foes.

Slag reined supreme. From the look of it, the guardian was not overjoyed to have so much moonlight in its eyes or on its skin, and the creature grew ever fretful. In a demonstration of renewed fury, it finally grabbed the next best thing to 'Salspear, the Peddler': the Konar himself. The creature dragged him with his looping tentacles back toward the mausoleum and scooped up his two closest cronies screaming at the top of their lungs. There was quiet then, and Risgan hopped the wall.

* * *

For hours Risgan wandered about, empty-hearted, wondering what had happened to Ravenna. Was she crushed under the broken columns in the rout? Had she escaped the Temple of Vitus? Did she wander alone in the forests, cold and disheartened? Had she simply died trying to contrive an escape from the despicable Konar and his regiment, perhaps even despatched by him at an earlier time? His heart fell at the thought of her demise. Risgan's imagination roved. His questions were various. They ate away at his vitals, until finally he contemplated sneaking back to the temple, only to assuage his doubt.

He did, drawn by his lingering dread. Nothing was left; the monitors had all fled, the acolytes were dead or scattered; now the site was a ruined mass of smoke and debris. Ravenna was nowhere to be found among the rubble. Somehow the observation comforted him. It was a cursed place, this Vitus sanctuary, forgotten and abandoned like the castle of old Hagus not far up the hill. Ever did an eerie pulse emanate from the moss-ridden mausoleum where Slag doubtlessly had entombed himself with the Konar.

The relic hunter retreated from the sorrowful place, aware now of how the world had come to be filled with such broken, mouldering ruins, the product of such entities as Slag.

* * *

A week later, almost by chance, Risgan heard a familiar laugh at the village of nearby Nufol in the back of the taproom of the *Singing Dragon*. A raven-haired maid pressed a polished fife to lips with a zither at her side. She was entertaining a crew of wayfarers who had gathered in numbers and clapped and eyed her with admiring approval. Risgan felt jealous at the attention. She was a charismatic beauty, ostensibly a changed woman, clad in a different garb now: of red skirt, white blouse and black-checkered shoes; apparently she revelled in assuming a completely different identity.

Risgan was astounded at the transformation. He could only stare with amazement. His heart surged with foolish pride and admiration and warmth. At a lull in the music, he took opportunity to approach her and draw her aside. With a tinkle of laughter and a sparkle of eye, she appraised Risgan and his roguish frame.

"You are looking younger and fresher than ever, master Risgan, though a trifle strained." Her gesture was playful, yet affectionate as she read the silent inquiry in his eyes.

"I try my best," responded Risgan stiffly. "And a pleasure it is to see you. I have searched high and low for you—under bush and over dale. Where have you been? Why did you not wait up for me?"

Ravenna croaked out a carefree laugh. "Dreamer! The temple grounds was a deathtrap, plus I thought you devoured by Slag. The compound was in disarray; the underworld minion was unleashed and seeing you alive now, I wonder how you magically escaped."

"'Twas not easy," admitted Risgan with a careless jerk of hand. "Slag was a sentimental sort. He wished to see more of the world and I obliged him. How fared you with the Konar?"

Ravenna gave a scornful chuckle. "I fear the Konar's vulgar exertions earned him significant grief. He sent away his henchmen and thought to entertain me with his largesse, neglecting to recall, as I remember, that I too was trained in the arts of self defence. Now, the dear Konar walks with a limp and may have trouble performing vigorous acts in the future."

Risgan chuckled and nodded. "That is not all he will have trouble with. Come to think of it, I don't find the incident implausible. A fitting punishment for our dear Konar. Though I think where he is now, there will be little chance of his performing new forays upon young acolytes. That said... as to our alliance and future communion..."

Ravenna's lips moved in a cool smile. "I shall entertain fond memories of you, Risgan. But we cannot be together. I have my music and much treasure to live on, thanks to the Konar's chalices. I managed to steal a few while he was indisposed. He shan't be needing them. Farewell, relic hunter, I shall remember you always."

Risgan gaped, stunned. "So, you're discarding me after all that we have shared?"

"All that we have shared? Is it not obvious? You are far too young for me, and somewhat naive. I desire a more experienced man, someone older."

Risgan croaked. "Someone older?" He could not quite believe his ears. Sensing the ironic thrust of the situation, he stewed over how handling the dark kraken-fired side of the youth talisman had made him younger. He debated toying with its aging potential to make him 'older' again, but then remembering the grim fate of Lubdar, he quickly abandoned such a plan. He trooped over to the bar to buy himself a stiff shot of arrack. When he returned, Ravenna was gone. A sad part of him knew that the only place he would see Ravenna was in his dreams, which would be lonely ones at that. He overestimated her impressions of him, and he underestimated her needs from him. It was then Risgan knew where he had seen the acolyte before. She was she mirrored in the face of a younger dream figure of the past—far way in the wastes beyond Fiffiholth—his alleged daughter, Ravel! Ravenna was none other than the mother of his upcoming child...

3: DIHBAS

After many adventures, Risgan felt inexplicably drawn to take the slow roads south, far away from the memories of his loss of Ravenna and what might have been. He intuitively chose a route devoid of hardship and intrigue, a route which took him closer to his native Zanzuria.

Risgan was much of a changed man, somewhat more weary and cynical, after his dealing with so many rogues and villains. However, he was even more youthful, courtesy of the youth talisman he had dug up moons ago in that lonely grave east of Zanzuria—always his sole noteworthy possession, aside from the Konar's sceptre. He clutched this enigmatic talisman like a hawk—and more often than he cared to admit. The beguiling light from the nephrite shell still mesmerized him: its dazzling blindness gave him youth, and its inky underside gave age and death, but a darkness sprang from the magic, a promise of untold peril, worse than any he could unleash by simply jettisoning it in the river, or a deep pit.

The relic hunter was not afraid to take such major roads at this time, feeling confident that his notoriety had died down after all these months. Winter was coming and the trees had turned a solemn yellow and grey. The north winds blew with a vengeance, casting chills over the lands, tendering him a dim feeling of melancholy.

Closer to his old haunts, Risgan decided to don various disguises, in the precaution of averting potential recognition. He embraced a false beard, a quirky hair style braided in the manner of the desert men of Zanthia; even the addition of a pronounced limp whenever it suited. During such moments of impulse, the treachery of certain persons in Zanzuria who had brought about his outlawed-ness, came back to mind.

With this dissembling, Risgan looked up his crony on the east side of town—Replex, a certain brown-bearded entrepreneur, owner of a high wide face and bright black ferret eyes. He was known as a competent contraband smuggler.

Replex met his colleague with merry cheer, seeing through the disguise at once. "Risgan, is that really you?" Replex looked up from the dim confines of his cluttered workshop with puzzled delight. "Old hog!—while we're getting more grey hair and grislier, you are getting more youthful!"

"Must be a trick of the light," remarked Risgan.

"Whatever it is, you have my envy! Well, let us retire to the *Gambler's Post*; we will share news over a pot of ale. This den of mine is glum enough. Look at all these stripped scimitars I must wrap, and erotic devices I must bundle up carefully in bags of sand. The officials at Zanzuria are a sceptical, conservative lot. We have much to catch up on..."

"Nay, Replex, I have other business at hand. I feel less festive of late."

The smuggler accepted the admission with a restrained sadness. The two talked of old times in low voices. "Haven't you heard?" his friend chuckled. "Farella is officially the new queen and is now ten years younger. Her divinator said she's regressed to the age of a sixteen-year-old."

"Is that so?" Risgan's eyes widened in surprise. "A strange event. So, Farella's a queen now?" He kept his tone even.

"Ever since old Pantius took a turn for the worse and accelerated his own age into his dotage. So mysterious. Now she's been sworn in to the royal hall, to rule Zanzuria, until young Eustan comes of age. What a piddle! The Pontific's little more than a geriatric now, the result of some foul spell, I hear, and the Divinators say that he's cursed. While you, my crafty chum, seem to share the same fate as our blessed queen! How can you figure that? 'Tis a better fate than the old Pontific's."

"Quite likely the canal water he drank," Risgan suggested. "Where is that swine, Vosta, by the way? Is he up and about, lapping at the swill like his henchman, Mistis?

"Vosta is here as always—at the market."

"Of course, I must pay Vosta my respects—I couldn't think of missing an old acquaintance of mine. It will not become me to be unsociable."

Replex fixed his comrade with a glassy-eyed stare. "You cannot mean that?"

"I am a changed man, Replex. First, I must make contact with another confidante..."

"So many friends and confidantes you have, dear Risgan!—even after your long sabbatical, and your history of pranks."

"I am proud of my achievements."

Taking his leave, Risgan secretly sent a message to queen Farella, saying that an old 'contact' with a 'fountain of youth' was back in town—that he would like to re-form an acquaintance. The message was delivered in earnest and answered, and a similar note sent back by envoy writ in a feminine hand.

Risgan's heart leaped. His brows arched as he read the instructions which bid him to drop by the palace at half past noon. Of course, Risgan felt a certain leeriness, even an anticipation, but he knew he was hardly recognizable being the wry young age of a smiley rogue half his years. He decided to risk the rendezvous.

Two men-at-arms accepted Risgan at the gates and escorted him with special care across the moat and through the high halls of the Pontific's pride. Gold and amber jewels glinted from above, dimmed in the lateness of day. Risgan thought it years since he had last set foot here, with the most unpleasant of consequences. A host of jarring memories flooded back while he followed the attendants through the old, lofty halls, who remained ignorant of the fate he had long ago walked into.

A private audience with the queen was not to be taken lightly and here, Risgan was well aware of it. He was admitted punctiliously to her study. He saw a plush set of divans, a purple-draped entrance to a boudoir, curtains threaded with gold, a gilded flask of wine on the table of carved wood. Farella stood before her divan, as stunning as ever, dressed in plush yellow gown and opulent emerald necklace about her neck. She appraised him with a glance of impudent curiosity. Indeed she was younger! Her chestnut hair shone with a lustre of the demiurge; her slightly oval eyes glinted with the most luxurious gold; her poise was as vivacious as ever. She fashioned small movements of arm, hand, hip, breasts, anything to beguile him, as she had done at an earlier time, sauntering now close, to face him with a brazen heat. Her slim shoulders were sculpted to perfection, her tall stance ever the same; a peach-pear complexion, redder than usual which set her apart from women her age. Her fantastic figure was ever heart-stopping, though perhaps a trifle leaner than he remembered, and, as Risgan remarked, had the uncanny way of riveting the most abstemious man's attention.

"Ah, Relic Hunter, you return. What news bring you?"

Risgan felt he had nothing to lose and in a moment of caprice, held her close. "Fair Farella," he whispered gently in her ear, "you must lift the oppressive bounty from my head? 'Tis inconvenient to stroll about the squares in this infernal disguise, knowing I could be seized and have my head lopped off. Do you forget who it was who gave you that extra ten years of life?"

"I do not," the queen replied graciously. "Since it was in an indirect sense, I, who made efforts to acquire it. I could still have you whipped for your disobedience and sent a hundred miles away."

"You could," said Risgan stiffly.

"Relax," she chuckled. "I am only learning the art of intrigue in a very slow fashion. 'Tis not as difficult to rule after all, or as sordid as I imagined." She gave a shameless giggle. "I hope that you and I can continue our associations in less scandalous manner, now that the Pontific is... well, let us say, indisposed. As you can guess, Pantius is a rather dull sort, at least in the arena of love."

Risgan mustered a hopeless grin. "I suppose it happens to every man at one time or other."

Farella waved a hand peremptorily. "Enough. And where is this bauble which I instructed you to retrieve for me?—the one that tantalized my eye so fulsomely long months ago at the market?"

Risgan sighed. "I threw it in the Badan; the jewel had an unwholesome hue to it."

"You did what? You fool!" Her grimace flashed unpleasantly. "Recover the bauble, or I will not lift your outlawed-ness. In fact, I will have you imprisoned. You have one week."

Risgan gave a terse objection. "The water is dark, populated with threlkoids."

"This is an incidental fact. Is this not what you do, 'retrieve'?"

Risgan growlingly admitted the truth of the statement. "I shall plumb the river," he grumbled peevishly. Again, he made the sign of the pact-warding charm behind his back. "Now that we are settled—"

"We are not settled. Not until the bauble is in my hands will you get any favours from me." She snorted. "And what good is your word? What of the Pontific's gold you accepted without fulfilling his commission, or failing that, never returned?" Her blazing eyes became a harsh sight.

"The sack lies at the bottom of the river," Risgan muttered delicately, "another regrettable accident."

"Ah, so many regrettable accidents... you are a clumsy fool! A stubborn and pig-headed man. If I didn't take a fancy to you, I would..."

"Yes, I know," the relic hunter sighed heavily, "I would be counting sheep in your donjon. But, I have other resources at my disposal: my good looks, and my good luck to repair this deficiency."

"Do you now?" she snorted mockingly. "Then, let us not delay engaging in these boons then." In haste the two settled down on the queen's divan to pass several hours in leisurely comfort—catching up on old business.

* * *

A few days later, Risgan, settling in at the inn of the *Wandering Wayfarer*, smoothed out his cheeks. Farella's threat, of course, was pure bluster. In time, she would realize her own folly and forget her desire for the nephrite. In the meantime, he prepared himself for his next coup. Using his skill as a connoisseur of disguise, Risgan proposed a minor auction at the High Market in Victory Square, mixing in of course, relics which he had unearthed and gleaned at St. Vitus's temple, along with the youth talisman. The rogue had secretly disguised the latter with a coat of red pigment and standing on a shabby podium, he presented himself as an elderly peddler, an amusing misfit of beggarly appearance, who had chanced on a trove in a faraway land.

Mistis the magician, casually strolling by the vendor stalls, halted. His ears perked up like a foxhound at the first mention of 'curios', for he was a coveter of long lost periapts and always on the alert for talismans that could better his magic. The beggar's descriptions of the modified youth talisman stirred hints of a familiar dark talisman and intrigued him. Risgan recalled the precautions he had taken to coat the bauble with the red pigment dredged from certain sand pits not far from the Badan river. He had mixed it with oil and tar to create a thick grit.

"Aye, Mage," Risgan called grandiosely, "one can tell only by stroking the lustrous contours of this crimson bauble that it is a rare item indeed."

Mystis rubbed his chin. He thrust out a heavy hand, to stroke the object as if it were an old habit of his to not show his ignorance. "Still, Monger, I am not impressed with the look of such an item..." His unpleasant grin spoke volumes in humouring an old shabby fool. "But the sceptre of this high priest... it indeed guards a heavy weft of prayer magic."

"That it does, magician, that it does."

Long ago Risgan had removed the hypnotic globe from the sceptre's pommel for a future occasion, and was not distraught in its loss even if it were sold at small gain. "A certain St. Vitus's magic infuses it, if I'm not mistaken. Hours of devotional prayers emanate there—all suffused into a single waft of potency. Look! I have seen it with my own eyes. On those travels north I witnessed marvels, in lands you could not dream of, Wizard! Some of the temple stations have shut down in the north, I hear, owing to a disaster at a central temple. Items as these are now verging on collectors' items." So Risgan went on, finally to state that it would be hard, if not impossible for him to sell the item cheaply.

The magician snorted in dismissive fashion. "Possibly so," he clucked, "but this should not be a factor in determining the price of the sceptre at any rate. There is always my hex of bad luck to consider."

Risgan paused, grinning wryly. "True." He bowed, deferring to the magician's wisdom. "You are a wiser lord than I, Sir Wizard. And I will not argue the point."

"See that you do not." Mystis showed a faint trace of satisfaction. "This is the way I do business, and how transactions should be carried out between wizards and peasants."

Mistis snatched at the sceptre and tossed a measly five mezks at Risgan's feet. The relic hunter bowed and gratefully accepted the bounty.

What luck! The relic hunter snarled a grunt of inward cold revenge. The vulpine fool had unwittingly stroked the down-curves of the talisman. Now Mystis would feel the taint of age. The magician had not bothered to scoop up the relic so that left opportunity that he might foul Vosta with it too. What a pretty unfolding thus far! Douran was shining brightly on him...

* * *

Recalling the trader Vosta's words so very long ago about how he would ultimately steal the talisman and snatch the wealth for his own, Risgan gave a malicious guffaw. Vosta was a true fool. He knew nothing of the relic's evil. No doubt, the relic was cursed—and no good would ever come of its use. How fitting then that it should be used as an instrument of vengeance in bringing about the trader's downfall!

With wolfish anticipation, Risgan washed the youth relic of its red stain, and for perhaps a last time peered upon its mystical contours. Smearing the dazzle of its convex with a resin from the butter-oaks, he dulled its brilliance, taking care to cover his hands while doing so, lest he pollute his already stable youthing while following a similar procedure to lighten the murky age-giving curve. Risgan camouflaged the dark side with a similar veneer.

At the end of his handiwork, he donned a different disguise—this one an old soldier with one peg leg and sword at his side. He approached his enemy at his kiosk in the central market of Zanzuria. Mistis the mage was nowhere in sight, a good sign: likely nursing his own troubles around the curse.

Vosta the tradesman leaned over the counter of his vases with frowning face. Lamps, coins and curios lay in an untidy sprawl to the side. Eyes glittered with interest at the bauble that the old soldier had to offer in way of trade. As was his greedy habit, he attempted to cheat him of a fair price.

Risgan, aka Hofta the soldier, gave a bereaved groan. "I am low of funds and must sell all my wares at a discount to feed my starving boys. Ah, you drive a hard bargain, Trader! but what's an old man to do?"

"Nothing, old man, now take your coins and buy yourself a watered grog."

"That's kind of you, sir," said Risgan.

Vosta grunted. "Hold up. Why do you wear such heavy mitts in such ham-handed way?"

Risgan looked about as if nothing could be plainer. "'Tis winter and the air is unseasonably chill. I must hide old battle scars." Risgan found it hard to bridle a laugh as he hobbled away, nursing a contemptuous exhilaration, as he turned to glance back at the avaricious vendor with his hands curled about the cursed gem.

A wail of grief escaped the trader's lips shortly after, when he realized what he had touched—the cursed entity that Mistis had warned him about. A small tremor of retribution tingled at the base of Risgan's spine... He rounded the corner to the *Golden Gibbeth*, discarding peg leg and false beard and trudged nonchalantly away.

* * *

Upon the fall of his enemies, Risgan was well to make himself scarce. Zanzuria would be a hot spot for some time, owing to his recent exploits. No matter. Revenge was a dish served cold. His only regret was the distance from his lovely Farella—and ultimately, Ravenna whom, he dearly missed.

His journeys led him to the same place past the mossy stone guarding the realm to lost Utreach, there at the ruined worship hall of Lin. How long ago had it been? Months. Why had he come all the way back here? Risgan did not know. Nostalgia? The end of a circuit? Drawn by old memories, patterns, a lonely spirit? It was the same place where he had discovered the fateful relic in the first place, hidden amongst those dank roots and earth in the mouldering sarcophagus.

Everything was as before: silent, lonely, eerie. The wood stood at a bowshot's distance from where the slavering gibbeth had pounced on him and almost gutted him. The mound he had dug into, had refilled with wet soil and was hardly the rude pit of old that he had hewed. Risgan surveyed the half eaten porphyry columns with a sardonic recollection; the broken overgrown pathways, the mossy slabs and the statues—all were nearly the same as he had left them. His expression remained unchanged—wry and thoughtful. He felt his smooth skin, ruddy cheeks, and sharp chin; his whiskers were ungreyed and now shone with a golden brown. The reverse aging may have run its course and he was struck with a new wonder and gratification. Finally the process halted at what he believed to be the young age of twenty five. Yet, the relic hunter was glad to be rid of the ill-fated artifact. The curse seemed to have lifted, and now new recipients would carry its burden.

Risgan felt his fingers twitch: why then did he still feel the sudden urge for the bauble?

He laughed. Unslinging his pickaxe, he began his usual probing for relics at an auspicious area not far from where an out-of-place granite slab cast with cursive runes teetered eerily out of the rank soil.

Time passed. Risgan's thoughts wavered eerily back to the nephrite gem, the time when he first discovered it—the sultry scintillation, the otherworldly pulsing, the mesmerizing glory of an age long passed. There it was again, that unnatural itch. What lurked beneath his fingertips? Did he hear the low screech of an isk from not far away?

The relic hunter paused, nursing a grimace. He shook his head in solemn wonder.

There would be other places, other times. Not here... this place was cursed. With a last look back, he gathered his gear and took his practiced feet southward to the land of Dihbas.

THE BONES OF ST. ISIS
(bonus content)

Bimsby—the 'rat-digger', and I, were supposed to raid the scholar's home and be in and out with his treasures in less than seven minutes. Easy as pie, Bimsby had boasted.

Bimsby was wrong.

All I have to show for it is a tale of ironic woe and humility.

I was a young man then, no more than a thin-faced street thief haunting the docks of Luxe for easy marks. Bimsby and I were legally commissioned by the Anti-Hexers' League to scout out magic-makers and curse-layers—we also pocketed whatever valuables came our way as a result of our 'excursions'. Why shouldn't we? We were legitimate members of the guild, I, 'ensign muskrat', my partner, 'rat-digger' of status not much better than my own.

The scholar's damask curtains were peeled back, showing a faint band of moonlight; the window was latched, though allowing an inch of air from the garden court.

My cutting tool was ready. We had climbed up the outside stairwell to look into the our mark's residence. But Bimsby in his fumbling haste, had gashed his forearm and roused the old man while cutting the glass to his bedroom window. He bolted upright in his bed like an eel. He rolled off his bed, twitched and rattled some nefarious 'objects' in his palm. It was a pair, actually a trio of *relics* in his gnarled hand. Which looked like bones.

He legged his way around the bed like a hare, baring his dagger, gemmed and embossed, snatched from the little night table. In his other fist he clutched these precious bones, hand-carved and multi-faceted. He let them rattle noiselessly on the pallet, then he looked at us with a meaningful purpose. The *Three of Mings*, the floating cube of *Suirs*, the *Moon Mogul*. I could see the archetypes clearly etched on the bones—but what did they mean?

The old man studied the darkness with that focussed scrutiny of his ilk. Shrewd, intelligent eyes of nearly 73, becoming apprised of two burglars lurking in the periphery.

Before he had let the ornaments fall, he seemed to size us up, as if he had some inside knowledge of our characters, some special power by which he could divine our inner workings. Those cursed runestones or *whatever* they were: he jiggled them, tossed them from hand to hand, all with a superiority—they had something to do with this reading skill of his. On closer inspection, they formed a perfectly cut set, embroidered with jade, possibly lapis lazuli. Even though the old man looked as old as death, he had a full head of white hair; he was equipped with surprisingly rich features, freckles and liver spots splashed all over his cheeks and brow. The details were branded into my brain under the eerie light of the candles which he kept burning through the night.

My initial consternation passed, I jerked to action.

My fool partner in crime, filchpurse Bimsby, decided to jump the gun. He charged the man.

Bimsby stopped dead in his tracks. The old man whispered something in his ear—a name—Zabele, or something. He hissed out some words which I did not quite catch—something about a pact with the devil of hearts.

I knew not what frightened my comrade so much, outside of a knowledge that there existed a certain Zabele, a high-order peer of the Anti-Hexers' Guild. But Bimsby made a sudden leap for the window, damaging himself on the upright shards. Indifferent to his pain, he vaulted down the stairwell and was gone.

I was left alone.

The scholar snatched up one of the circular relics. His eyes seemed to glow all over, following my every movement.

I was frozen with fear, and yet even if I wanted, I could not budge. He was harmless, this benign old man, but one who had frightened one of the unruliest thugs in Lux, and with no more than a few arcane objects and a whispered word.

The miraculous man reached for the cabinet; I was sure he was about to snatch for a dire weapon, but he fooled me—quick as an adder, he dove under the bed. In those two seconds he held up a real weapon—a well-oiled musket, armed with a double shot and aimed right at my chest.

I understood then that I was no hero.

The scholar smiled, his face crinkling into a snakeskin grin as he tossed the weapon aside.

"I have no need for this beastie!" he cried. "Bah, the old thing is antediluvian; it will jam on the first knock. Milly the Magician could not make it fire."

Blinking away my confusion, I pondered the truth of his statement. The scholar's act of putting the gun away, astonished me, thinking that I, Paspon, junior muskrat, thief and uncoverer, would neither harm nor bolt.

He seemed to know these facts. The man designed that I would attempt nothing more witless. Honestly, it annoyed me.

I deigned to speak, but he held up a hand. "No words, lad. We must be out of here. Hurry! I'm sure your charming friend will return in no time with other strapping colleagues of yours."

There was a frankness to his logic. Why didn't he blow my brains out?—I was a thief. The deep empathy in the old man's eyes bespoke of a wisdom and compelled me to comply. It was the look that calmed me; his gaze did not allow me to look away, or think as I might usually—which was typically quite exceptional.

"Make yourself useful, boy!" he growled. "At least gather your cutting tool and your wits, rather than goggle like a cow. You'll need courage!" He spoke more briskly now, not nearly as sympathetic as previously.

"There may be profit in it for you," he added grudgingly.

As for these possible kickbacks, or curios, this hexagon, circle, cross and bones—inlaid with lapis lazuli and jade—I was at a loss. If I was meant to uncover such relics, as my guild demanded, punish the holder, I had failed in the task. The scholar seemed to read my mind, and beat my glance to the window.

"Since we're rather intimately involved, I'll let you in on a little secret."

"What is that?" I breathed.

"I'm originally from Parnoss, the city of the Magi, and I came here as somewhat of a refugee. Seeing as my cover is blown, which you have had everything to do with, wisdom demands action. I was planning to leave tomorrow, but it seems as if I will now have to hasten that plan." He studied me intently, like the bat that ogles the insect. He gathered his eldritch relics and clutched them in his palm very queerly. "There is a certain providence in this business we must pursue. Certain signs I have witnessed."

He drew a parchment from his night table, and drew back the curtains which we had rudely pulled aside.

The parchment was scrawled with a curious riddle. The text was blurred which he showed me: "*All daggers point to the same path. Where is the hope?*"

I was unimpressed with the puzzle—I had heard many of their kind, but he seemed to think it was the cat's meow.

"Ah, you wonder of my relics?" he asked brightly. "They are cut, polished, rubbed and set with the most costly gems. See for yourself!"—he held them up as if to tease my eyes with their strange opulence. "They are the bones of St. Isis, the patroness saint of the 11th century."

"They could just as easily be bear bones from the forest."

He laughed, but I shied back in fright, for my ignorance was astounding. These adjuncts had the reek of thaumaturgy about them. We were a superstitious people—we *Luxians*.

Sensing my immoderate amazement, he conferred a smug truth to me, "Don't dissemble with me. Now you know my secret. But know that all the secrets of the universe are writ in the smallest and subtlest of signals."

I professed that I hadn't the slightest clue what he was talking about.

He stepped away from the light. So did I, for I could see things better to the right of me, owing to my large eye patch.

"This future I see in you is very interesting," he mused. "What is your name?"

"Paspon. Who are you?"

"I'm Sir Glasmus of Parnoss."

"Well, *Glasmus*, what does all this talk have to do with me?"

"You are going on a very long journey, my young friend!" he declared with cheery energy.

"Really?"

"Of course!"

My inner musings ran about in highly objectionable circles. I balked at the possibility of any extended trek, but I found my reflexes not obeying my command. Probably very much in the manner that Bimsby had fled in the midst of a pressing, well-paid job. Yet I felt it was not the scholar doing it, but his wretched *charms*—or at best, his will, if I could be so grandiose to conjecture. I was not a religious man, so I could not wholly accept this latter reasoning, but I am only saying what I felt...

"These relics are the bones of salvation," he added majestically. "Toes, fingers, joints."

I frowned, not knowing how to reply. It was in my nature to regard inexplicable phenomenon with only contempt.

Of Glasmus, I knew nothing, other than that he was some scholar trained at Baxbury college in the early half of the century. The arts of astrology, physics, mathematics and philosophy were not unknown to him. He was rumored to be an amateur student of occultism, which unsurprisingly I felt was true.

The man was a physiognomist, a reader of people's faces, hearts, their deeds. By observing body-language, tones of speech, the all-round basic imprint on the air around them, he could learn tremendous truths. This, I was to learn after, for my intellect was not near the match of Glasmus's. He was a master of synchronicities of mother nature herself, reading all her phenomena as if they were pages from a book.

* * *

In the back room Glasmus briefly changed into another costume: an elegant doublet, a grey overcoat, expensive rabbit-leather gloves and high black knee boots. A huge plumed hat rode his greying head, which made my modest dockside, filchpurse-garb look flagrantly ridiculous. But he didn't seem to mind the clash and he urged us on to haste. His only unprepossessing quality was his front silver tooth, which marked him as something of a snaggle-puss.

We took ourselves into the dim-lit streets, cobble-slick from a recent rain. I caught the wink of Luxe's lanterns down by Smilly's dock. Our port was an orthodox seaside settlement—her stone and timber-framed dwellings hung a very long way up the hill, as they overlooked the sea.

Behind that knitted darkness I knew such contrasts as the decrepit wharf and her brothel-pubs, the relative opulence of the Tabernacle of New Hope's steeples, the inestimable Filchers' Guild domes, next to the low spires of her Holiness's Anti-Hexers' league-house. Of course, behind were the anti-curse temples, and the demon-spirit cages for those recently deceased who insisted on leaving their taint on the living. But I tried not to think of those profane places. How this *scholar* had managed to conceal his craft from the world and continue his hoarding of charms was beyond me.

The rumors of his wealth—and the clandestine proclivities he must have engaged in—they must have been well-masked.

A foghorn blew. Cinder-block warehouses stood out from the few residences; seedy inns on the harbourfront showed as checkerboard shapes. A sea mist chilled my bones, bringing me memories of my apprenticeship to uncle Jaffy who was elder fisher-master of the trawler *Wingsparrow.*

The lighthouse winked across the bay; Deadman's Isle, only a league out in the harbour, showed as a skeletal finger of rock. The lighthouse's feeble glow veiled in the mist did not comfort me.

We fled Luxe—meaning 'Luck Lack' in the old tongue—hearing the town bells striking one, prompting a dog to howl. But I did not feel any remote reassurance, neither did I feel in my proper skin nor any semblance of good will to this excursion. Everything around me felt as if I were seeing things in a heightened light, perhaps through the scholar's gaze, or his eerie rattling of those bones.

Glasmus plodded on in his half-hobbling gait, oblivious to my torment. He chided me for my brooding. He chattered on as if there was no threat, as if everything was as it should.

I began to grow restless. The truth of what I was doing, aiding and abetting a dissenter, was gnawing at my moral conditioning. Yet I was doing it, and something of the absurdity of it struck me as funny. Then I was caught in a wave of confusion, lightened only by the old man's banter.

We marched briskly to the next way-station where we might ride by coach to Dunhalter. However, there was no coach for the next seven hours. We decided to trudge it. It was no small jaunt, actually a four league hike, and unfortunately the old man's mention of a return visit by Anti-Hexers seemed to infect me with the jitters. Why his residence was the one Bimsby and I were slated to target, was beyond me. I was battling the sudden urge to bolt, fighting the compulsion to trot at his side and engage in his illegal escapade.

That this grey-haired 5', 7" plump little fellow could have such a hold on me was astonishing. He had forgiven me my trespasses and made me his associate in a matter of crime. Destiny seemed to weave strange paths for the least suspecting...

* * *

We caught an express coach by chance, flagging the vehicle down on a deserted cobble road to Litchvoy. The driver let us out at the junction to

Kerk's ferry. The coach, driven by a mettlesome team of stone bison, was a fast rider. The one-horned, caparisoned creatures never tired, even though they were fed little fare.

Glasmus paid the coachman eleven silvers and the coach disappeared in a cloud of roiling dust; it headed west to the old stone fort high in the hills of the Mason uplands bearing the flag of 'Ronan', proctor of Dion. Beyond, the road dwindled, swerving to Aramon. Dawn was in full swing and windmills dotted the countryside: rolling lands, quiet yet reticent, contrasted with the distant hill forts. Prayer wheels rattled in the nearby field, competing with the goatbell chime of ruminants, grazing in the riverside pasture. The residents of Dion were no less devout than we of Luxe.

The ferry was nothing more than a sizeable raft with low wicker railings pulled by roped harback-oxen. We crossed the sluggish waters and Glasmus paid the ferryman his fare.

We had gotten no more than a mile up the old Axon road when two disreputable brigands came stumbling out of the heather.

The rogues had been lurking in the weeds for some time, judging from the smell of their jerkins. They must have stolen a purse, or robbed some gentleman's wallet, for their sneers were evident and the clink in their pockets suggested skulduggery.

I caught the whiff of ale as they clambered in front of us, looking like Denkie's crowd from Dockman's Pub, but they weren't—for their faces were too hatchet-like.

I gave them a menacing appraisal.

"Becoming a turncoat are we, Paspon, dearie?" the foremost man said. "I think Bimsby will like our report—about how O'Flassery and I discovered one feckless traitor dallying about with an old hexer."

"Aye," his mate laughed, "your old codger must have some real stash to have jumped town so quick."

"Mind your tongue, oaf," I warned. "We are sojourners."

"Sojourners, are you? Well—" he ripped out his rapier, which sparkled silver in the daylight.

"Gentlemen!" interrupted Glasmus sombrely. "Let's have none of this uncouth bluster. We are sensible beings."

"Shut your trap, you old fool. You have what Hektor and I want. Give it to us, old man, quicky-pie, or we resort to bloodshed."

"'Tis an unreasonable demand."

"Relics are forbidden in Luxe! You know it. All are worth a king's ransom, so—"

"Us being thieves," Hektor persisted, "and members of the guild—"

"We are not in Luxe," I blurted out.

"Mere details," asserted O'Flassery with a huff.

"How did you find us so quickly?"

"We have our spies."

O'Flassery waved a hand. "We were sent by Vomey, head of the Filch Guild in our neighbourhood. He got word to our Anti-Hexers by local carrier pigeon. Fancy that!—a brilliant piece of technology."

"The system is somewhat archaic," I muttered.

Hektor's blade came streaking out. I raised my cutting tool to thwart the strike but—

I had this yellow patch over my eye, as I have mentioned, and I could not see straight—depth perception being my weakness. The injury I received from a dirk in my face one late-night on a street-filching gone bad. For this reason, I was not Glasmus's best choice of a valet, whatever he expected of me. But foes have a habit of underestimating my dexterity and tend to fall victim to my tricks.

Not this time.

The rapier came sliding down the haft almost shoring off my thumb. The goats munched noisily nearby, blinking at our distress.

I loosed a painful gasp.

Sensing that we were on the verge of being spitted, Glasmus put out a comradely hand. "You should know, gentlemen, that's not the way to conduct parley." He wagged a jewelled finger. "The process of synchronicity is very scientific and one based on the Y-Mng philosophy, steeped in the mystical arts—but you, being gentlemen, should know that."

The two halted their blades and exchanged baffled looks.

Glasmus flourished one of the relics. "A very plain person sees only bits of porous calcium here, or jewelled bones there, yet a percipient person sees marvellous tools. He watches all the movements of the universe, however small. He sees the mysteries of life, the conjunctions of action reaction, thus they are explained to him in simple fashion: he acts with acumen; his actions which reflect every outcome and happening, are his teachers. The hypothetical person becomes a veritable expert, an observer, a discerning paragon, much aware. He sees it in the rise of the sun—the lilt of the plants, the turn of a mishandled weapon, the faces of the exposed stone, the direction of the winds, the quality of the moisture of the air, the attitudes of the planets, the moods of the individuals around him."

"Very pleasant, old man," growled O'Flassery. "But we do not have time for folklore."

"You are busy men, I know," said Glasmus with a sigh. "Eager to spill guts, but hear me out."

Hektor made a complaining gesture. "Why not? Shall we humour the old goat, O'Flassy? Are we in such a great hurry?"

"We have money to collect, and a slaying to do!"

"Ah, first things first, my dear man!" cried Glasmus in mock exasperation.

"I am curious," Hektor cried. "So indulge me."

The scholar gave a rueful shrug. "Like now, for instance. Your peer has gone very red in the face. This occurrence tells me that his impatience has mastered his limited intelligence. He bluffs his way by hiding something important from you. A conspiracy? Transgression? O'Flassery now has his sword gripped in a very defensive fashion. Why? The quick thrust in the throat, the collection of a sole reward? He has fidgeted with his pommel a dozen times now for no explicable reason. Is he hiding something from you, Hektor?—a treachery, a lie—perhaps a false-hearted motive?"

Hektor jeered at his mate. "Well, then, O'Flassery—let's have it, ye backstabber—"

O'Flassery went very pale; the scholar noticed his Adam's apple bobbing up and down, and I noticed a bland smile creeping over the flush of the scholar's lips.

O'Flassery whirled on the scholar. "Fink! Tell him it's not true."

Hektor rounded on his traitorous chum. "What's this? Some truth behind the old goat's claim?"

O'Flassery, not knowing how to respond, flushed crimson.

"You lily-livered hound!" cried Hektor.

Out came the villain's sword. A flash of steel and a clash of blades caught me off guard and I started to sway, understanding some of Glasmus's wiles. He was a marvel of truths, a reader of possibilities, a facial analyst. The blasted bones heightened his eerie perception!

We scurried away hastily. I turned a glance over my shoulder—saw O'Flassery slash out at Hektor. A carriage was rattling down Taulle's way.

Hektor used the opportunity to hip check O'Flassery into the oncoming vehicle.

Now the wheels made short work of O'Flassery's torso.

Hektor was left staring at his mangled chum. The carriage had not paused to assess its damage, nor was Hektor in any condition to come hobbling after us.

Glasmus's ploys, though innocent, seemed ruthless. "A bit inelegant, Glasmus, but effective all the same," I remarked.

Glasmus gave me a nod. "'Twas a spur-of-the-moment gambit."

"How did you do it? You have this Y-Mng capability then—"

"Oh, Heaven's no! 'Tis all bluff."

The pause in my response prompted Glasmus to smile impishly. "Truth can never be concealed, at least for very long. Everything that is suppressed rises to the surface, like flotsam on a filthy beach."

"Very philosophic."

"This is the reason all humankind will never be completely lost," he explained matter-of-factly, "one merely has to open to the reality and look, if he dares."

"Very profound," I muttered.

"I knew you would understand. So, shall we? I fear the day is wearing."

"You still have not explained to me the Y-Mng synchronicity—"

"Ah, must you be so tiresome, boy?"

I shrugged in exasperation and down the winding track we went to the next town, called Axon.

* * *

At this distance from Luxe, I bore witness to the strangest boats. We stood before the crescent harbour of Taulle, about thirty leagues from Kerk's ferry, watching hulls outfitted with Danngs' wings tilted on an angle and in such proper winds, to race over the swells as they entered port. The wings lifted the hull several feet above the water to make riding the rough waves easier.

We took passage aboard the *Rainbow Rider*, a beautiful three-masted, lateen- and square-rigged caravel, light as air with her white, shimmering Danngs' wings. Her scallop sails, hemlock masts and spidery rigging made me quiver. Surely she was one the finest sailing ships of her day.

As for payment, Glasmus appeared to have an adequate supply of silver stashed on his person, for which I was grateful. I would not have had this privilege otherwise and it spared me the tedium of thieving for bread and cheese.

We took ship to Hasfmus, a town seventy leagues to the south-east as the crow flies. The caravel fought the trade winds. At her forecastle I caught glimpses of the wild isles to starboard with stark, gull-haunted cliffs reaching into the Messany's blue waves.

Glasmus came secretly up behind me and touched my shoulder. "It was said that the islands are homes to the people of Cristos. Holy people who could transform themselves into birds, fly from isle to isle—travel the distances to the neighbouring islands, congregate and share lore."

I drew back, pondering the truth of it.

"No lie. Somewhere it was said that St. Isis herself came from the sacred island to the left; she flew to Parnoss of the Magi where she strove to enlighten the people and convert the indomitable Magistrar to the true path of the cross."

Glasmus grumbled sadly. "The mystic failed. Now her bones adorn my pocket. An irony, no greater than the Magistrar's evil which fashioned these bones into a cross, carved by the artisan himself."

"A prickly fellow, this Magistrar."

"Indeed."

I shivered, chilled by the bite of the winds.

Glasmus remained indifferent to my unease and glanced idly at sombre crew who worked the wind-weathered deck. "These bones are cursed—and blessed, by St. Isis. She was gifted in the powers of prophecy."

I could hardly fathom such marvels and I nodded in slow apprehension. What dark mission was I on with this enigmatic man? "Are we going to visit the Magistrar?"

"Yes."

"If I had of known—"

"You would have refused?" Glasmus grey brows lifted in merriment.

I resented his mocking reply, yet could come up with no rejoinder of my own.

Glasmus went on: "I was entrusted to carry out my master's last wish. These bones were his gift. For over twenty years I have attended the Magistrar's Masquerade, hoping to elude his cunning and crack his riddles."

"Where, at this ball?"

"Oh, no ordinary ball is it!" cried Glasmus. "Once a year, he holds it, to see if any clever person can solve his obscure puzzles. A whim—a ceremony which he performs with elegant grace each year—for his amusement. No one can crack his riddles; they are indecipherable."

I snorted. "Anything can be cracked, unlocked. I should know, I am a thief."

The mates thought it odd that a young swain would be attending so old a man, but Glasmus quickly assured them that I was his ward, a precocious teen who, having little taste of the world, needed a fresh perspective. I coughed at the stretching of truth, but I said nothing—I was, after all, given a free ride. The sailors accepted the master's account, but wondered how much of this old minister's wealth they could sap before the trip was over.

At first Glasmus refused to participate in the gambling but then he reluctantly acceded to their invitation to a round. Below decks we crept, down to the lantern lit gallery where the sailors indulged in their games, unknown to the captain.

I watched the play for a period, after which Glasmus piped up, "Good show, quartermaster! You deal a fair game but in a very roundabout way. I suggest a more innovative approach. How about like this?" He took up a pair of skewed dice and tossed them flamboyantly on the gaming board. In his other hand he wielded the bones and I could see that they infused him with a sort of flush-faced thrill, and magical advantage.

The dice showed clearly the double knaves of Ming and caused the quartermaster to cry out.

"You're a bloody misfit! But I like what I see. I'll not refuse a challenge. Here Carpfin, you old dog. Pass me my six bits!"

Carpfin did not enjoy the quartermaster's tone, but he put his hand on his marlinspike. "The devil I will, Blistin! 'Twas not your throw that won, 'twas clearly the old man's and only a test."

"Nonsense! Hand over my wins, before I clout you. That's twenty bits you owe me!"

"And you, boy," jeered a deckhand at me, one with big red bandanna on his forehead and slick black teeth. "What conjuring do you bring to this table?"

"None," I confessed, waving a trembling hand. "I must admit that Glasmus steals the show."

The boatswain did not argue. Carpfin refused to relinquish his silver bits and there came a quarrel which grew to a brawl and which ultimately escalated into a melee which we took care to distance ourselves from, and we scrambled like rats up the companionway.

* * *

Glasmus was in good humour, but something seemed to be gnawing at his liver, perhaps something to do with the bones, what he had seen in his wild tosses, which he rattled off regularly in the stateroom we booked. Indeed, I had never tasted such luxury.

"Normally," Glasmus mused, "by the falling pattern of the bones a person infers happenings, signals of things to come, or what are presently in motion. But again these are impossible to quantify for reasons of the subtle nature of the universe's ways."

He threw down the bones.

I could see that there was a peculiar accent in the way they fell, and judging by Glasmus's wide, trembling eyes I guessed that there was much omen in the interlocking configuration. "Hai!" he groaned.

"What?"

Glasmus sighed at my ingenuousness. "Every year I go to the Magistrar, hoping to unlock one of his infernal riddles, but I always come away disappointed! Bit by failure! This time, I see no better result."

"Very good, master Glasmus, but how does that involve the likes of me?"

"You shall help me decipher his riddles."

"I?" I quivered absurdly.

Glasmus gave a low bow. "None other! It is for this very reason that I brought you. To divert his suspicion."

"It sounds like a ridiculous longshot."

"Ah, it is not. The Magistrar has eyes of a bloodhawk, his senses are attuned. If he gets wind of our collusion, then we are finished."

"Why then do we try?"

"Do not trouble yourself with that. It suffices to say I saw it in the bones."

The comment irritated me for whatever reasons, but I stayed quiet. I was indebted to the old scholar; somehow he had not done me any harm, a gift which still perplexed me.

* * *

As Glasmus explained, Parnoss was once a fief, but now an indentured territory, ruled by the questionably-benevolent lord the people called the

Magistrar, a *vice-roy* as he had clarified, who had established a colony of lawful burghers. For this reason, the Magistrar alone had built the most opulent manor of the city, on the northern boundary of the old Magi acropolis.

Parnoss was far away from the *orthodox* realms—Luxe and Taulle and Aramon—and as we were to see, had no such inhibitions of magic as we Anti-Hexers in backward Luxe were accustomed.

Spirit dancers caroused in the streets, crafting melodies on their harps and lutes, drawing magical entities from the air like fireflies to manifest into physical form. The dancers' assistants trapped them in glass cages for a short time, before releasing them in the air, for Parnoss was a free territory, and magic was permitted. The crowd was pleased.

What wonder! I could see the sprite-like faces pressed close to the glass, making faces, resentful of their capture but given to outrageous antics, while others of their kind hopped and skipped, performing jocular demonstrations within those bottled cages.

I was taken aback by the thaumaturgy and somewhat repulsed, owing to the conditioning of mine which I could not shake. Glasmus seemed unperturbed, and to treat my consternation as an amusing study. He responded in kind. "My bones seem not so bad after all, eh, Paspon? Now you see why I fled to Luxe. To escape the Magistrar's persecution. He is a lord of eeriness. He does not wish to journey to those territories which are so averse to magic. He would cringe at the sight of our hidebound spirit cages and our anti-hex leagues."

"I don't doubt." My eyes glazed over, staring at the old Magi acropolis and its sister ruins tumbling down to the seashore.

* * *

The ball was open to all. Residents of Parnoss poured in by the dozens to loiter at the Magistrar's great gathering hall. But only the most affluent and prestigious would gain entry. Nobles and delegates and certain privileged merchants. How we were to gain entrance to the event was beyond me, but Glasmus was a remarkable fellow—and it was a masquerade after all.

We purchased our costumes at the local haberdashery. Dusk had fallen. The businesses were well equipped with fabrics and finery.

I was dressed in an impeccable captain's costume, wearing high-peaked buccaneer's cap with skull and daggers decked on my crown. Glasmus dressed as an aged mineral prospector who sought to surprise with a turquoise scarf wrapped round his wig of thick grey curls.

We arrived at Moonsmith estate—for that was the Magistrar's title for it—a blackstone manor fashioned after the robber-barons of Old Parnoss. Our arrival was late and so the footmen were already less vigilant. Eccentrically designed, the residence boasted a conical fore-tower and larger keep crowned with a giant black cross in the shape of an inverted cone. To the sides, three pikes lanced up—of what appeared ships' masts. The effect was quite dramatic, if not unnerving and I decided not to inquire of its significance to Glasmus. The last light was failing and we hustled down the tree-lined lane with urgent hopes.

Portentous hedges surrounded the residence, one leading to an abominable maze, a vast topiary, I discovered, which dizzied the eye. An eccentric garden peeked from its manicured edges. A small wood reared at the back, curling in an aspect of darkness which brought little comfort to my soul. Many warm lights flowed from the casements. The sounds of women's laughter drifted melodiously from the portals, high, bright, gay sounds, infusing us with cheer.

We proceeded past the iron gates and up the walkway. An elegantly-attired gentleman met us, directing us into the foyer, where we took our time adjusting to the warm light streaming from the parlour.

A hundred or more individuals were gathered, in fantastic costumes: hunters, wardens, balladeers, magistrates, fools, blacksmiths, blackguards.

One damsel caught my eye and made my throat leap. Here was a slim huntress dressed in soft brown leather and a small bow tucked at her shapely hip. Her gait was light, her face set in a infectious smile; her lips were thin and red, but her grace and intelligence bore a beauty that lingered in my soul long after. It would not be dismissed, though I blinked several times.

The host, or impresario, was the Magistrar—a tall, hovering figure, wearing the ornate headdress of a minotaur, black with silver tips set along its golden crown-piece. He wore it like a king, sweeping through the parlour with ceremonious grace.

"Welcome, citizens! Amuse yourselves well! Rejoice. Dance! There is plenty of time before my riddle-reading."

A flamboyantly-dressed poet took Glasmus aside. "Can it be? The famous Glasmus? This comes as no surprise."

"Tilnaeme—good to see you," the scholar acknowledged with affection. "But where is your crony, the good Baron Bloss?"

"I'm afraid the Baron lost an arm and a leg on a bears' hunt midsummer's eve."

"How frightful!"

The topics did not interest me; and so, I was not sad to see Glasmus taken away.

The huntress was beautiful—more than a stunning jewel to my eye. She had a vivacious ease to her every move. Her words were like psalms to my ear, tinkling whatever need be said over the ballroom's vastness. Would that I was a gallant lord and not some lowly thief! I would have wooed her off her feet and taken her as a bride! But that reality was non-existent; I was what I was, and destiny would have its way.

I turned my attention to the Magistrar.

He spoke of his deeds with boastful ease—how he governed the province, and levied the taxes, and adjudicated the law. He held a sceptre which he brandished like a monarch, adding weight to his pompous convictions with thrusts and little twirls. To my ear, he seemed full of hot air. He kept motioning to a large drape configured at the side of the hall, which had some mysterious thing hid, doubtless the thing which had to do with his 'riddle-reading'.

Despite his arrogant airs, I felt something untoward about his address, but I was not so subtle to pinpoint it. Glasmus gripped my elbow, steering me to the refreshment table, as if to keep me occupied, but I could not resist the sight of the beautiful damsel, whom I learned was Comptesse Lady Tessa de Vailley, and when there came a lull in her line of eager dance partners, I snatched up the chance, asked her breathlessly for a number. I felt myself awkwardly blushing as I bowed, waiting for her answer.

She did not decline; a curious smile afflicted the corners of her lips. "Your colleague Glasmus, moons over you like a pet mastiff! I have seen him never like this. I have seen him many times, but you?"

"We are newly acquainted, Glasmus and I. Bosom mates. I am—or was—a fisherman, now I am more of—a *valet*."

"A valet?" She seemed bemused at the admission, but also charmed. A person of my bearing actually daring to ask a comptesse for a dance was something peculiar.

I hardly cared, for I could feel my heart thumping—no it was pounding!—I had nothing to lose.

"Ah, I see you have met the Comptesse," the scholar squeaked from behind me, with sly interest.

"Indeed, sir. And I was—I mean, we were about to—"

"Dance?"

"Yes."

"Master fisherman. Shall we?" prompted the comptesse.

I glanced back at Glasmus, giddy with rapture. Again, that sad fatalism in the old man's eyes. What was going on in his head? He tried to put on a cheery face but it didn't fool me. He had witnessed something in those wretched bones.

I had other concerns at the moment.

The Lady was soft in my arms; her body was the warmest shield, I was floating on my heels.

"I don't believe you've mentioned your name?"

"Paspon, my Lady. Sorry, I apologize sincerely!"

"No need! You are a curious fellow, Master Paspon—so modest and tender in your speech. Yet you seem to have dark edges quivering around your soul. What is it? A battered crow seeking to claw itself out of his nest of thorns? It is as if you've been some sort of vagabond criminal in this past life."

I grimaced at the allusion; it could not help but make me cough.

She gave a lively chuckle. "Well, if you have anything to hide from me, Paspon, tell me now!" Your accent is strange—lilting, like a Dunhalter's. Are you from around there?"

"Actually, from Luxe. I'm Frejian."

"Indeed!" The conversation continued like so, and I, lay clearly besotted by this queen of the valley, verily spilled my guts about myself and all I knew about Luxe and my current travels, but I left out the part of my thieving, mentioning instead only my extensive fishing career with my uncle.

Whether this route was wise or not, I had not the chance of knowing, for the dance ended and the lady was off, attending to her many other dance partners.

I left giddy, feeling dangling—slightly breathless, and somewhat empty and weak of knee and heart with a pallor I rarely felt. But cold to my stomach, as if the absence of her warmth pained my insides.

The hours passed by quickly. In a whirlwind of flashing smiles, glittery teeth, jewels, touches, gestures, hot chandelier light, urbane laughs, the string ensemble's lulling harmonies did not help my swoon.

Through all, I had the grace and comfort of the comptesse's gaze which settled on me twice, and I even came to experience a flashing of her kohl eyelids and a speaking of pleasant words to me, which soothed my heart much.

When the riddle-time finally arrived, I was ill prepared.

The Magistrar waved his sceptre, created a dashing fireworks that filled the upper galleries, igniting it in plumes: cherry, red and plum apricot. There were coos of amazement, sparks and ribbons dissolving into harmless streaks, and people clapping for more firework tricks, but the Magistrar shook his head. He held up his hands in a manner of polite forbearance. "It is time for the ceremony!"

Composing his words, he boomed, "Long ago, a priestess was sent to convert me to the white faith and I was disturbed by the audacity, and have placed my indenture on you who allowed it! . . . Parnoss shall not pass away from my scrutiny until such time as a clever citizen solves my riddle. Once a year—three chances are given to lift the indenture—so did your governor Gwalen of old, sign the document in his own blood." He reached fastidiously for his breast pocket, withdrew a yellowed parchment, which showed the crimson streaks of the governor's bloody seal.

Lady Tessa had wandered close and wiped away a tear from her cheek and whispered in my ear. "The Magistrar is mad! Tsar Kurthe fears him, so do his advisors. So has the Tsar allowed him to continue his insolent viceroy-ship over our territory, even though the governor's days were numbered over a century ago."

I croaked. "How old is the Magistrar?"

"Do not ask."

I was expecting him to read from the parchment some fancy epigram, but instead a lackey swooped out from an adjoining chamber and uncovered a genie's ball hidden at the side of the room behind that massive drape. A pure crystal piece it was, graced with shifting images that coalesced from iridescent metallic speckles. All guests blinked, and studied the phenomenon with awe.

The Magistrar closed his eyes; suddenly the speckles moved to the tune of mental images. Fabulous scenes—white swans paddling on a golden lake, twin moons setting over a twilight forest, rainbows arched over an older Parnoss, lovers entwined in abandon in an enchanted bower, a treacherous kiss, a tryst involving a magic broach intended as a gift, a castle under siege, a kingdom on fire! The magic was such that the Magistrar could merely think the image and the liquid would obey his command. The immersed speckles in the crystal were straining the limits of animation, creating the impression that he desired—an old thaumaturgy whose mechanics were lost in time.

Another image flashed—something akin to an old wooden gate. Dark ravens flew over it, a small sinister November wood huddled to the side.

The Magistrar's glass ball continued to shift ever more diabolically, into detailed, unsettling variations of the scene.

The host's voice pierced the silence. "So, who will try first? You Casgale? What is beyond my glass? I have written the answer on this flash card, so there can be no doubt of chicanery. How about you, Glasmus? Your disguise is paltry. Don't pout! Anyone can see through your ridiculous costume. Every year you come to make a remarkable contribution, which is inconveniently wrong."

Glasmus made a strained shrug. "I am no magician like you."

"An honest man!" the Magistrar cried out jauntily. "Who will try then? Our barber then! He seems the mettlesome sort."

"Heaven's no!" cried the barber.

"Then who?" the Magistrar cried unpleasantly. He tapped his foot like a disgruntled count. "Come on now! We haven't all evening."

At that moment, the scholar shoved the bones in my palm.

I looked at them in horror. I tried to return the cursed things, but Glasmus shrank back and have nothing of it.

It was the bones in my hand which gave me an unconscious view of the Magistrar's mind. I gazed in awe at this impertinent figure. A nobleman, yes, but every stress and weakness in the lines of his face I could read—the sneer of his teeth, the malevolent droop of eye.

This was some sort of foul magician, perhaps an impresario of style, imbued with a fancy pride, a mysterious prestige and expensive habits, owing to high letters and a position in society. But here I saw him in his true light—a master manipulator, an affable snake, a deceptive patrician, holding everybody's interest in mind, but none to heart. He appalled me with his clandestine guile. Without these bones, I would never have seen the marvel of his duplicities so clearly—but now I knew!—I thanked Glasmus profusely with a side glance, of which he was keenly aware.

I perceived too that the Magistrar, in his flagrant pride, had not bothered to create alternate cards to refute an answer, should one of the guests guess accurately. My penetrating insight grasped all this, and I registered it with outrage.

Glasmus glanced at me with alertness. I could not read what it meant.

"Incorrect! Next!" came the Magistrar's humorous, mocking shout over the anguish and disappointment of the crowd.

The Magistrar announced. "Well, citizens, it seems as if two have failed. You are no better off than last year. A single guess—to remove the thrall of your territory!"

"You are harsh, Magistrar," cried one who was the chancellor, a thick-bellied man dressed in a humble woodsman's garb.

"Give us more chances!" cried Parmella, the first lady to Duke Calhil.

The Magistrar tugged at his goatee. "Never! My decree is final and my program is immutable! It seems as if one more guess shall decide the fate before the year closes, with yet another luckless pass!"

All the time a strange compulsion had been coming over me. My lips registered words of whose meaning I had no idea. Glasmus detected it; I sensed that I would waffle our final chance at victory! He croaked out impatiently. "Wait! Let the young lord speak."

The Magistrar turned and stared incredulously. "Young lord? Him? What would he know?"

"Much!"

"The foreigner is a mere stripling."

"It is not explicitly forbidden that foreigners may not guess."

The Magistrar wrinkled his nose. "So, then, on with it."

Glasmus urged me to respond. His gentle eyes touched me with an inexpressible fire. "*You have the bones. I cannot use them. The bones whispered to me that I cannot guess.*" His hiss barely registered in my mind.

Lady Tessa urged me on; her soft hand touched my wrist and ignited me with passion. The bones turned sideways in my hand. The riddle came to me in a split of a second.

"A raven with one eye cannot seek a gate, unless he has two peers, but he can always count on one crafty squirrel to fly high through the knothole—the squirrel, ha!—somewhat like myself."

I giggled, blushing, thoroughly embarrassed at what I had just said.

The response seemed to upset our host. He faltered, levelled a cold glare at me. Enraged astonishment stuck in his throat; a red flush gushed over his proud face.

"There is some trickery about here!" He bored fish eyes on Glasmus. "You!"

Glasmus looked away innocently.

"So, the answer is right then?" cried Tessa. Overjoyed, she jumped up on the balls of her feet, clapping her hands. "We are free then!"

"No, you are not free!" the Magistrar called. "There is more to it than that."

Lady Tessa fumed, hands on her hips: "Paspon deserves his dues. Give it to the young man. Where is your honour?"

"Honour? This bumpkin hasn't the brain to guess any of my secrets. They are impossible! Decryption is hopeless!"

There were unsympathetic grumbles from the crowd.

A shout lanced from the throng: "So what have we here?—a dupes' gathering, a sham, a continuance of your hold over our province without judicial mediation?"

The Magistrar grinned. "If this is how you would think of it, then yes. All this moribund talk—let us speak of other matters—like how these two imposters have sidestepped my rules. They are fraudsters."

"It is you who is the fraudster," called Glasmus. "In admitting that you rigged the riddles, for failure."

"Nonese. You are your accomplice shall be punished. Harbouring inside knowledge of my riddle is a felony."

I denied the allegation, though I knew it was not entirely true, feeling the uncanny warmth exuding from Glasmus's bones.

Tessa cried out unheedingly, "My father, Tsar Kurthe's treasurer, is not without his influence. If he were to whisper word to his sire, perhaps your smug little kingdom would be less—"

"Silence! Your boasts are poignant, lady—but deeds speak louder than words. Can you back up your claim? When all is done, who shall bear witness to any crimes today? Every one of you are cowards . . . oops!" he moaned in mockery. "The answer card has slipped from my grasp—It has fallen on this hot lantern wick. How careless!" The yellow parchment sizzled on the nearest candle flame. "How are we to know the real answer?"

There were vicious reproaches from the gathering.

Almost on an unconscious level, the Magistrar flicked eyes to the chandeliers with a mirth. My keen eyes saw the movement, I read his mind—it grappled with a chance—that his scheme would somehow be exposed.

I shuddered, my mind reeling with a brief glimpse of the synchronicities that must endlessly surround poor Glasmus's mind while wielding the bones.

I could see the Magistrar in his true light now: an evil manipulator—a forger of the bones of St. Isis!

Glasmus had made himself vulnerable in his role. Why? He must have seen omens in the bones. Was this his final fear, a fatal confrontation with the Magistrar?

The Lady Tessa berated her host. "I beseech you to return the old man his honour and the youth his prize! You are not true to your word."

In rage, the Magistrar ordered her apprehended. The lackeys seemed well-conditioned to the task, securing her with cool efficiency. She was detained for 'belligerence', taken into a side room by the servants for a dressing down.

I made efforts to club those arrogant lackeys with my false cutlass, but I felt rude hands pinning me from behind. I was frog-marched off the premises, to the Magistrar's infamous garden. Glasmus tried to protest but he was seized too, and painfully taken below.

The townsfolk were irked, appalled by the arrogant treatment of their citizens, but few of them spoke against the Magistrar for they feared his fey powers. The few who did, including the chancellor and Duke Calhil, were threatened at swordpoint. The Magistrar's valets contributed to their seizure. I, who was nothing to them, was gagged and blindfolded and thrown into that infernal maze, the 'topiary' but not before the lackeys twirled me like a top till I was dizzy. I called them blackguards and swine and every foul name I could think of, but the exercise was in vain. I was thrust rudely into the maze's prickly confines. The guests were herded out into the chill air.

They set to torture the old man then, whose dreadful screams I could hear faintly from the open window to the cellar. The agony! Hearing those appeals and knowing that this kind old man was under such undeserved duress set my heart into a tailspin! I was helpless as a fawn, trapped in an eerie labyrinth. But I pooled my resources, thought of the lady, of everything I could, pouring over all that the old man had taught me—on the ship and passing the hundreds of leagues.

I ripped off my blindfold, set about examining my prison. It was more ominous than I had imagined, stretching as far back into the corridors of the woods as could be imagined—I was about to try scaling one of the thorny flanks but desisted, sensing the futility of the task. The walls of the shrubs stood twelve feet high, and waxed three feet thick—too formidable for one such as I. But I had the bones!—not that my feeble skills could do anything with them.

Footprints? The ground was shot with many of them on the short springy grass. The turf left no indents. Driven to despair, I found at last that climbing the rampart was impossible—too sharp and springy, thick as a herringbird's nest. Attempting to cut through the brambles only tore my clothes and pricked my flesh.

Magical stuff! It must be composed of vile material. I grimaced, disgust dribbling from my mouth—my inclination toward unnatural phenomenon was clearly aversion.

The moon finally rose, a synchronicity that saved my spirit—for its humble disc showed light where there was only darkness.

But the mist and air seemed to belie the direction of the scholar's outcries, and hence the manor—I was ever the more befuddled. Curse the Magistrar's magic!

I was prompted by an inordinate stench to back away fearfully. I nearly stumbled over a bulky, shattered thing.

To my further dismay, research revealed it was a a half-decayed corpse in the bend of the topiary. Obviously some poor wretch had not succeeded in finding a way out before starving to death. Like me, if I did not get out of this foul pit. Devil! Who could perform such feats?

The Magistrar.

I forced my eyes to peer upon those horrible remains—remnants only of a clue I sought, but there were none in that tortuous labyrinth but more forsaken bodies. Rattling the bones in my palms like Glasmus did, I hoped for some miracle—as if the blessed St. Isis would rise up from her grave and give me some shelter!

I read by the angles of the corpses, the specific branches and avenues they had tried and had failed. It was writ in the skin-riven grimaces of horror, the fright and the agony. I was white as a ghost after scanning but not without hope; I chose those dark twists and eerie, taunting curves that led the way out of the maze.

Into the salon I crept, catching a glimpse of Lady Tessa. She was detained beyond a glass of double-doors by two lackeys whom I recognized from before. They contemplated her with lust—it was no secret. My fingers knotted into claws. The bones bit into my flesh.

A cry drifted in tragic synchrony—Glasmus's! From below.

I grimaced, with indecision gnawing at me. Tessa would have to wait—I must deal with the scholar.

To the foot of the stairs I hurried, cringing at what I must do.

The sepulchral chamber lofted high in chill shadows; I entered with no enthusiasm. My feet found a dark, warped stairway, and my nose gagged at the repulsive reek.

Adorning the walls were torture instruments, many of them. Shrivelled ugly heads, hung grotesquely, embalmed by some sort of obscure thaumaturgy.

"Ah, Master Paspon," came the Magistrar's voice. "Glad you could join us. I see you balk at my décor. Pity!" He had just lifted his minotaur's head from a sprawled human mass that was Glasmus on the torture rack. "Yet it does not surprise me. You are here, having escaped my ghoulish maze. You are a man cleverer than I thought. What's this? You bring me my bones! Naïve of me to have thought that Glasmus would have them on him. I grant you every right to chide me!"

I had no patience for this rogue's quips, and I rushed in, breathing raggedly, shouting hoarse threats at him.

He ignored my diatribe. "As you will observe," he explained, "your master is soon dead—unless you hand over the bones."

"These?" I held up the trio of cursed things, wanting to shove them down his throat.

"Of course, what else would I want? Your blessed shoes?"

I had nothing to add and firmed my lip mulishly.

The Magistrar then ripped off his infernal horns and brought out his shiny rapier. "As you wish, coxcomb. Prepare to die! But of course—you have nothing to draw with!"

He lunged, nearly stabbing his point through my heart. But I was quicker, and had not indulged in alcohol, like many of the persons at the masquerade.

The old man looked dead, impaled on the torture rack like a sick deer.

Two silver forks protruded from his abdomen, akin to a sort of abominable acupuncture. His eyes were peeled back, forced open with toothpicks, and his face was set in a rigor-mortis of agony.

I reeled with disgust.

"I regret to say," quipped the Magistrar, grunting as he lunged, "that Glasmus's divination exercise—or shall I say exorcism—has failed."

"You are a degenerate lowlife!"

The Magistrar breathed a fretful sigh. "What can I say? I am not always the man I seem, nor am I liked by everyone. Success is not always measured by words."

I boiled with anger.

"Do not listen to him," Glasmus moaned feebly.

He was alive!

"Flee, you artless fool! He is beyond you," moaned Glasmus. "You cannot save me!"

"I will not desert you!"

"Master Glasmus, I bid you to quell your tongue before I carve it off with this bodkin—" and the Magistrar gave one of those eldritch forks a tweak and struck out hard on the knee with his blade. I heard cartilage crack.

I seized a twisted skewer from the torture wall and began to hack at the Magistrar. He laughed, darting back, jeering at my efforts, pleased to know that any depth perception I had must be very minor with the patch over my eye, and would pose him no hindrance. He began toying with me like a mouse.

"Come now, little grouse, come get your seeds."

The nobleman was a more experienced fighter than I, and with the inferior weapon I held, things were not going well for me.

His sharp blade tore at my breeches. He jabbed, cut bloody swaths in my ribs while I blundered on without plan or program. My clunky manoeuvres were ill-wrought and my skewer was ineffective. But there was one single advantage I commanded—that I held the bones—perhaps my last departure of irony.

Glasmus stirred, his eyes flashing on perhaps one last gruesome sight. "Oh, shades!" he cried feebly. "You tacked my master's head on your loathsome walls—wretch you are! Poor Senestus, my dear master."

The Magistrar only gestured in perfunctory fashion.

I looked with horror to the place where Glasmus's eyes rolled. A shrunken puppet of a head pinned upside down showed no eyes or teeth. The punishment was symbolic, as if the Magistrar were the weigher of persons' souls.

"Yes," sighed the Magistrar. "Old Senestus and I had been friends before we turned rivals. He thought I was too much of a pompous dark magician for his tastes. Poor devil! Senestus had discovered the secret of the Y-Mng. Clever, but in truth, they would not serve either of us, though they were essences lost for centuries from the mystics of the far east."

"You stole it from him!" grunted Glasmus weakly.

"Not before the buffoon had hidden it so deeply in the Mirror of No Return, that I could not find it!"

"You got what you deserved," croaked Glasmus.

"Perhaps. But I created the riddle sequence from its shadow, its secret withheld, only using a small facet of its true power. Aye, this business is a bad one." The Magistrar smoothed out his goatee. "But life is like that. Some lose, some win. I think I can safely say that I win—" he grinned meaningfully.

"Your callous indifference is unspeakable," I cried, redoubled in my fury.

"And who cares what you think, little pipsqueak? Soon you will know the true meaning of pain. Oh Parnoss, why am I even bothering to tell you? I'll have the bones—now!"

Glasmus gave another sharp moan.

I used all my powers to try and better the situation, save poor Glasmus. If I could only see through this villain's defences! Fiddling with my trembling hand over the bones, I saw an image appear in my mind: a weak-kneed fool with wooden braces lining his shins and knees.

The knees! So that was it. The magician had weak knees—a sense of false assurance too, the flip side of an excessive pride.

I lurched over to the stairwell and lured him to the short flight of steps leading up from his den. I lunged when he was on the last step. A slip, a tumble and the villain's knees buckled as if signals were sent but not received.

I surged forward, despite my bleeding ribcage. The Magistrar tottered, fell two steps and I ran him through the gullet. He fell, beeding out on the stone, choking out a gurgle.

I raced over to Glasmus and the old scholar was in bad state but I gingerly removed the wretched forks from his abdomen, carried him up the steps. "Take the bones," he whispered. "Use them for greater purposes." I heard his faint wheezing cough rasp to bloody foam.

"But I know not how to use them!" I cried, grief-stricken.

"You will." Suddenly Glasmus's hand fell limp on my wrist.

I laid him at the top of the landing and scrambled away, glad to be out of the odious chamber, but heart-pounding, I searched for the means to commit my next move. I gained the Magistrar's study, crept to where the lackeys held Tessa. They were laughing, having their sport with her, almost stripping her naked, when I came blustering in, holding Glasmus's bones, swinging my skewer.

They quailed at the sight of me. I was alive—how could that be? None escaped the Magistrar.

They fled in terror at the obscene condition of their master, glimpsed briefly from the landing, no less the naked fury of my vengeance.

I released the comptesse from her bonds; she hugged me till I almost felt crushed by her embraces. As for Glasmus, well, I tried to save him, but he'd stopped breathing a few seconds ago. The lady knew something of the healing arts and ran to obtain some healing salves and unguents from the kitchen, but it was too late, for the scholar died in my arms as she rummaged.

I lay crestfallen, defeated, an empty shell of a man washed on a bleak shore. But I had solved the riddle; Glasmus's quest was done. I had avenged the scholar, even rid the world of one malefic foe—but from the bones in my hand and the sight of the sweet lady's eyes, I knew my true destiny had only now begun.

ABOUT THE AUTHOR

Chris is a prolific author of fantasy, adventure, and science fiction. His writing spans many genres: heroic fantasy, sword and sorcery and speculative fiction.

You can connect with Chris at:

http://www.innersky.ca/booktrack

www.ingramcontent.com/pod-product-compliance
Lightning Source LLC
Chambersburg PA
CBHW051841170626
46807CB00003B/1282